One
Fatal
Night

One Fatal Night

HéLENE FERMONT

A CIP catalogue record for this book is available from the British Library.

Paperback ISBN 978-1-9163543-1-9

E book ISBN 978-1-9163543-0-2

I dedicate this novel to all wonderful people whose lives turned out to be different from what they believed was true. Always remember no one and nothing are what they seem. In the end, what matters most is what we make of our own lives.

My gratitude to all my readers whose kind reviews and comments mean a lot to me.

And to my special friend, Lena, whose friendship inspires me to never give up, no matter how hard life can be at times. You are my hero.

Last but not least: To my gorgeous, loyal, affectionate cat and writing buddy, Teddy, who sits next to me in his old wooden box while I write. I could never be the determined, passionate author of my novels and stories without my darling fur baby.

Let the novel commence. I hope you will enjoy reading it as much as I did writing it.

CHAPTER ONE

DANIEL HOLST COULDN'T take his eyes off the curvy blonde in the corner of the dimly lit foyer on the ground floor of the hotel. He'd decided to attend the celebration of the annual Enterprise Award for Best Business Achievement despite what had taken place earlier that day. Taking a sip of the lukewarm white wine, Daniel decided to throw caution to the wind and walked up to the blonde.

His face was so close to hers she took a step back. "Are you who I think you are?" she asked in a sultry voice.

Moving closer to her, he said, "That depends. I can be whoever you want me to be, honey." He pulled out a card from his inner jacket pocket and watched her face fall when she read the name.

"You're Daniel... Daniel Holst? But I've n-never met you before! I've worked upstairs in accounts for nearly two months... How come I've not met you until now?"

"I don't normally attend these functions. But tonight's special, so I decided to make an appearance."

Daniel cleared his throat and took a closer look at her. "What's your name? I'm not personally involved with members of staff. That's Joel's job." He liked the fact she knew nothing more about him, except that he was her employer.

"Joel Wranger? He's your deputy manager, right?" the girl asked in a shy voice.

"That's right. Joel's my right arm. We've known each other for years." Daniel omitted telling her Joel was the only person who knew everything there was to know about him. If for some reason, Joel decided to spill the beans, Daniel's life would be open to scrutiny. He'd put his past behind him and had no intention of going back. Neither did his old friend.

Setting her glass on the windowsill behind them, the girl sighed. "I shouldn't speak out of turn; it's probably the wine talking. I've had too much to drink. But I don't like him. There's something about him that gives me the creeps. He keeps asking me out and I keep turning him down. But he still undresses me with his eyes. I feel nauseous when he comes near me."

Brushing his arm against her long hair, Daniel sensed she was brighter than all the other girls working for him. "Is that right? Perhaps I ought to have a word with him?" Watching her eyes fill with dread, mouth trembling, he added, "You needn't worry that I'll reveal your name. I'll just bring to his attention that several members of the staff mentioned he's too... what's the word? Too personal for comfort."

Daniel reached for her hand and looked into her eyes, his lean body and her curvaceous figure fit together nicely, but she pulled back a bit.

"You'd do that for me?" she asked, staring into his eyes. Like so many other women in his past, he could tell she was attracted to his blue eyes, handsome rugged face, and short white hair.

"In a heartbeat," he said. "I'm pleased you're not intimidated by my presence. What's your name, honey?" He deepened his voice and held her gaze.

The girl hesitated briefly and then replied, "A-Astrid Jensen. I've left Bergen to come and live and work in Oslo. Getting a job here is a dream come true for me." The words tumbled out quickly and then she put a hand over her mouth as if she wanted to stuff them back in.

Eyeing her up and down, Daniel smiled and gently touched her face, replying, "I sense there's a connection between us. Let's meet up for a drink. How about we continue this conversation later tonight?"

The girl turned to pick up her glass from the windowsill. "Perhaps. Why don't I give you an answer later? I've never seen you before and rumor has it you prefer your own company.

Surely, someone in your position would prefer to spend the night with friends and colleagues?"

Shaking his head Daniel registered her words and slowly took a step closer to her, his hand gently touching a strand of hair falling into her eyes. "Nah, that's not my style. With my commitments and business taking up all of my time I don't wish to spend longer than I have to with other people. You and I, we're two of a kind. Tell you what, think it over and let me know later. I'll be at the bar waiting for your answer. And, honey, don't look so worried. I'm a big teddy bear deep down."

He took a step back and wondered what to say next to make her warm to him. "You shouldn't believe everything you've heard about me." He turned around and walked away, a satisfied grin on his lips. Astrid Jensen was just a pussycat. He'd had his fair share of girls like her, courtesy of Joel. It wasn't Joel she ought to fear but the man who was her boss.

Earlier that day a dead body had been dragged out of the Akeselva River, which ran through the city. Joel had seen to everything, assuring Daniel no one would find out about his involvement with the dead man. If someone found out the truth, his life wouldn't be worth living, and if Joel so much as breathed a word about it, Daniel would make sure he lived to regret it.

Walking up to the bar, grinning at the crowd, he smiled at them, shook hands and proceeded to order Champagne.

"Tonight's cause for celebration. I can feel it in my bones. Here's to Holst Enterprises, the deal is done. All we have to do is wait for the announcement."

Emptying his glass, Daniel looked around him at the cheering crowd. He'd come a long way from the humble beginnings of his childhood.

Putting his worries to the back of his mind, Daniel uncorked another bottle of Champagne and said, "Here's to everyone who worked their asses off to get where we are now!"

He heard a voice whisper behind him, "The answer's yes. I'd love to get to know you better. Why don't we go back to my place later?"

"Great!" He said. "There's something between us... Don't take this the wrong way... I know you like your job. I could tell by the way you sounded when you told me you work for me. How about we get to know each other better? I promise you won't regret it, honey."

His lips brushed hers gently, one hand holding the curve of her spine through the flimsy fabric of her short, tight dress, the other the glass of Champagne.

"Sure. I'll see you later. We'll continue this conversation then."

Walking away from him towards the dance floor brightly lit by spotlights, Astrid smiled. Daniel Holst, you don't know me, but I know you. When you think you're safe, I'll reveal the real reason I've left my old life behind. You'll never get away with what you did. Never.

Turning to look at the other people on the dance floor, she saw his eyes were following her every move. She raised her glass and blew him a kiss. So far everything was going according to plan.

CHAPTER TWO

ASTRID WATCHED DANIEL get out of bed and enter the cramped bathroom in her small flat. They'd spent the night together, and her entire body ached after what they'd done. She was convinced she would be the envy of his female employees if they knew about her and Daniel. But it was nothing more than a brief fling she had maneuvered to get close to him and execute her plan. A plan that had consumed her entire life and was the reason she'd relocated from her hometown, leaving behind everyone and everything that meant something to her, to start fresh in Oslo.

Hearing him sing along to some tune on the radio, taking ages to shower and get dressed, she stretched and yawned, then got up and put on an oversized t-shirt strewn across a chair by the window overlooking the shabby street outside.

You'll never guess what I've got in store for you, she thought, suddenly disgusted by what she had done last night. Daniel

Holst was a powerful man. He'd achieved everything by himself, the business, luxurious lifestyle and last night The Best Business Enterprise Award, which everyone had known was in the bag even before the winner was announced. Viewed as one of the most influential people in Norway with a huge personal fortune, Daniel had achieved what most people only dreamed of.

But the time had come for him to pay for what he did all those years ago.

Watching him come out of the bathroom, a big grin on his lips, she cringed inwardly when she heard him say, "Last night was great! How about we make time for a quickie before I leave? Joel's waiting for me at work… Apparently, a man's body was dragged out of the river. It's unfortunate for us that the incident took place so close to our building, but business comes first, even at times like this; you agree with me, don't you?"

Nodding, Astrid went up to him and took his hand in hers. "Sure. Yes. Let's have a repeat performance of last night. It won't take long and it will get you in the right frame of mind for work."

Hating herself, she closed her eyes and went through the motions.

Twenty minutes later, it was over and she felt relieved. She offered to make breakfast. "Coffee and toast okay with you?" she asked, willing herself to stay calm and focused.

"Nah, but thanks for offering. I'm late as it is. Can I ask you something, honey?"

"Sure. What's on your mind?" She felt queasy and desperate to wash him out of her skin and hair.

"How come you've got sleeping tablets in your bathroom cabinet? You're too young and beautiful for that sort of thing."

Anger welling up inside her, Astrid snapped, "What's it got to do with you? I'm an adult and do as I please!" She regretted saying too much the minute the words were out of her mouth.

"Of course you are, honey, but it's unnecessary to rely on tablets... Unless you've got an underlying problem? A sexy girl like you ought not to worry about anything. I'll get in touch later this week, we'll meet at your place and if you're really lucky I'll spend the night. Does that sound like a good idea to you?"

Seething with anger and eager for him to leave, she nodded, not trusting herself to not lash out at him once more. "Sure, if that's what you want... I've got to get ready for work; my shift starts in exactly one hour."

Brushing past Astrid on his way out, he looked into her eyes and said, "I had a great time; you're something else!"

Grabbing his jacket and mobile from the small table next to the bed, he disappeared out the front door.

As she sat alone in the tiny bedsit, Astrid's eyes welled up with tears. Wringing her hands, she ran into the bathroom and showered for nearly half an hour, her body shaking from the memory of what they had done. Scrubbing away his mouth and skin from hers, she couldn't stop crying and detesting herself for her part in it. *But it was necessary to prove how much I care.*

She dried herself with a big light blue towel and cleaned up after him, throwing her ripped, flimsy clothes into a bin outside the flat. It wasn't until she'd eaten a piece of toast and drunk half a mug of strong black coffee that she wondered, *Did you feel the same as me, Mor? Did you hate yourself as much as I do now? Daniel Holst has no idea who I am. I'll stick with the plan a while longer until he gets what he deserves. All I have to do is wait for his call and the next installment of what I've got in store for him.* She smiled and started to clear the table.

CHAPTER THREE

JOEL'S GUT INSTINCT told him Daniel wasn't pleased with him. Ever since the girl had applied for a position in accounts, Joel suspected she wasn't who she claimed to be. He'd spent too long cleaning up other people's messes to not spot a fake when he saw one. Astrid was pretty and polite, yet beneath her facade of innocence, he felt certain she was keeping something from them. He wondered what it was and how to find out about it.

The past few days had passed in a blur. When the homicide officer interrogated him and Daniel, asking if they knew the dead man, they had told him there wasn't any connection between them and the deceased.

Seated in his office, one floor below Daniel's penthouse apartment, exhaustion blurring his vision, Joel sighed. So far so good. But the officer who had interrogated them had a suspicious expression in his eyes each time they replied. It wasn't until they were on their way home from the station that Daniel mentioned his name. "Morten Knudsen has got it in for us. He's like a dog with a bone, refusing to accept we don't know the murder victim."

Feeling beads of perspiration on his forehead, Joel opened the bottom desk drawer and rummaged through the contents. He pulled out a gun in case it would come in handy. When that body was dragged out of the river, he'd been the police's first call, since he was head of security at Holst Enterprises and the body had been found near their property.

Getting up from his chair at the desk and vividly recalling the victim's identity, he whispered, "Elias Fleming. I always knew we'd meet again."

With anger, he remembered their first encounter in a bar where Joel had been serving drinks after he had moved to Oslo from Bergen. The nightclub was a trendy place for people working in the capital and criminals involved in shady deals and underground syndicates dealing in drugs and prostitution. Elias had recently moved to Oslo from Bergen too, and the two men had been socializing for a few weeks when Joel had offered the other man his living room settee to spend the night until he found a place of his own. The two of them spent every night in trendy bars and clubs. Elias was involved with fraudsters and gangs. It was hardly surprising he ended up dead.

The things he knew... I kept warning him to not take risks. Unlike me and Daniel, he was caught repeatedly by the police. I've got to make sure he's not linked with us. The slightest hint or trace and our past will catch up with us. Worst case scenario, who we were then will ruin everything we've achieved, especially Daniel.

Wiping the sweat off his forehead with his jacket sleeve, he cried out loud, "For Christ's sake, Elias knew the score." But he was too involved to get out. That girl... Astrid... She had applied for a job around the same time Elias called Joel out of the blue, asking to meet with him. He wanted Joel's help in some deal. When Joel declined to meet him, Elias said they were through forever.

Daniel's an idiot getting involved with that girl! I've got to find out more about her and the reason she's here. Pulling out her file from the top shelf next to his desk, he browsed the contents, eyes falling on her previous positions. Placing the file on his desk, head spinning, he paced the room.

He'd been right all along. Daniel's latest fling must have known Elias. He'd been involved with a woman in Sandviken, a Bergen suburb, many years ago. What if the girl met him then? Joel vaguely recalled the woman's name. She had been murdered several years ago. *Ingrid Jensen... It's a common surname. Could Astrid be her daughter?*

What was the connection? It was hardly a coincidence she had applied for a job here and become involved with Daniel.

He had to find out her secret and why she was here. When he did, he would tell Daniel. Until then he would tail her every chance he got. This was his territory, and Elias was murdered for something he did or knew.

Morten Knudsen informed Daniel and Joel that Elias had been beaten to a pulp and shot in the head twice, then thrown in the river where a group of teenagers discovered his body when walking home on Holst property after a party.

Joel knew only too well how shocked they must have been finding a corpse in the dark. He'd been only slightly older when he'd started to work for Daniel, making sure the past wouldn't return to haunt him.

Shaking all over, Joel asked out loud, "Why is that girl working here? Did her mother die because she and Elias had a fling?" Racking his brain, he suddenly thought of something. What if the girl had a grudge against The Boss? But why? Elias was dead. It was too late to ask him.

Clearing his desk, Joel turned off the light and left, exhausted and desperate to get back to his nearby flat. The last week's sleep deprivation was affecting his ability to think clearly. He staggered towards the back entrance, took the lift downstairs to the garage, vowing to come up with the answers he so badly needed to protect his friend. *I'll find out the truth about her.*

Walking to where he'd parked his brown Mercedes, next to the old station wagon he'd bought with his first paycheck in Bergen, he got inside and was about to drive out of there when he heard a voice behind him.

"You haven't figured it out yet, have you? You've really no idea why I work here?"

Turning to see Astrid sitting in the backseat, he asked, "What makes you think I care?"

After what felt like an eternity, she replied, "You ought to. Stop lying to me and pretending you have no idea what I mean!"

She got out of the back seat as quietly as she'd entered and walked to his window. "What goes around comes around. I'll deny our little conversation, but you'd better watch your back and not stand in my way or I'll make sure the police know what you and your friend were involved with!"

Watching her disappear from sight, Joel felt certain she wasn't alone. She must have found and copied his car keys. Astrid had an accomplice. He couldn't stop thinking about what they had in mind for him and The Boss.

CHAPTER FOUR

DANIEL AND JOEL were in his flat above Holst Enterprises, drinking wine and eating canapés delivered by the local delicatessen. Seated at the old wooden table in the kitchen, with panoramic views of the neighboring buildings, both men stared into space.

"What happens now?" said Daniel. "Elias and I hardly knew each other apart from the few times we met when both of us worked for the syndicate. And now you're telling me I can't date the girl? Astrid's just a fling, nothing serious. You know me, I never commit to anyone. She and I are just a temporary arrangement."

Wringing his hands, Joel said, "I've done my best to keep you out of this. It's only a matter of time before the police figure out our connection with the victim. It's a miracle he lasted as long as he did! I warned him this might happen, that his past would catch up with him some day. If only he'd kept away from that woman, it's a relief she's dead!"

"Are you referring to who I think?" Daniel asked. "But that happened such a long time ago. Surely you don't imagine her death is connected with Elias' murder? He was an idiot. The number of times you bailed him out when he got himself involved with someone. You and I had an agreement to never get emotionally involved. Even after such a long time, I recall how beautiful she was, yet also fragile and weak."

Daniel looked down at his hands, painfully aware of his part in her life. It dawned on him Joel knew more than he let on. Watching him standing with his back to the window, Daniel said, "You're hiding something from me. I'll sack you unless you come clean! You're nothing without me!"

Turning to face him, Joel replied in a cold voice, "Go ahead. If you sack me I'll inform the police of everything you used to do. If it wasn't for me you wouldn't be where you are now! Everything you've achieved is down to me just as much as all the hard work you put in to get this. This place and the business is our achievement. And this is how you repay me? All I ever wanted is your respect for cleaning up after you. I've kept a record of all the things you've been involved with. The police would love to get their hands on it! Perhaps I ought to consider it. They'd do anything to get all the gory details of Norway's most famous business man."

Laughing out loud, Daniel shouted, "Blackmail goes both ways! Did you really imagine I'd let you get the upper hand? I've kept my eye on you since the first day you started to work for me. Your weakness for young girls barely old enough to be your granddaughters disgusts me! I've got evidence of all the dalliances with underage girls, so don't ever threaten me again or you'll live to regret it, is that understood?"

Joel slumped down on a chair. "I tried my best to keep you and us out of it. Astrid's your biggest problem. She knows about our connection with Elias! Do you recall he wore a ring on his right middle finger? Knudsen casually mentioned it and said the ring was discovered on the common."

Daniel poured himself another glass of wine, drank it in less than a minute, and placed the empty glass on the table. "I vaguely recall the ring... What about Ingrid? How come you bring her into the equation? You think the girl's related to her?"

He poured himself another glass of wine. He'd spent years thinking about Ingrid, wondering what might have been if he'd not left.

"Finally, the coin's dropped!" said Joel. "Yes. Astrid is her daughter. Surely now you must see a possible connection between her working for you and Elias' murder?" Joel gave Daniel a hug. "We've been through too much to give up on everything we've achieved. Whatever that girl's up to, we won't let her ruin everything you've worked so hard for! Please say you'll end the affair. She can keep her job so I can keep an eye on her."

Downing his wine, Daniel paced the room. "You're wrong about her. So what if what you think is true? Ingrid died years ago. I cut my losses as soon as I realized how dependent she was on me. Every relationship she had ended the same way. No man wants to be with a woman who expects everything of him. Beautiful yet too fragile for her own good! In the end she suffocated me with her constant demands that I show her affection and abandon my dreams so I could be with her."

"I know what you mean but her daughter's hell bent on getting revenge on you and me for what happened that night! Just say the word, and I'll make sure she disappears from your life for good."

Nodding his approval of his friend's suggestion, Daniel suddenly changed his mind. "No. Don't look so scared. I want to know what she's got planned for me, us. You must go out of your way to be nice to her and pretend you care. Astrid can't know about her mother's involvement with our activities in Bergen; she was just a kid back then! All she probably knows is how unhappy and broken Ingrid was.

"We're the only ones who know the truth about what we did in those days. Unless... Elias told someone who in turn informed her. If she finds out what happened that night... It doesn't bear thinking of. I'll behave as normal and you'll do as I say pretending everything's fine. We've left that part of our lives behind and no one will ever get the upper hand on me. I'll make sure of it!"

If Joel so much as breathed a word about Daniel's part in all of it, he'd bring him down with him. Gesturing at the surroundings, he said, "We've come a long way from where we started. Ingrid was a fool for love. Her daughter's just as foolish, thinking she can get revenge on me. I've lived by one rule ever since we left Bergen: No one ever gets to me. Falling in love is a sign of weakness."

"I know, but Astrid knows something and she's blaming you for her mother's death. I feel certain she's got an accomplice who helps her. I'll not rest until I know who it is."

Taking a deep breath, Daniel replied, "Perhaps you're right. But no one knows about what we did in the old days. If what you say is true, someone must have been tailing us for years. I stick with my initial decision; keep a close eye on the girl but be discreet. I'll continue dating her and do my best to find out the identity of her accomplice. Neither of us laid a finger on Ingrid! After we left her that night, someone else must have turned up. I only found out she'd died before we moved to Oslo.

"I confess at the time I was relieved she wasn't a part of my life anymore. Her constant accusations and whining got on my nerves. Ingrid was a liability back then and by the looks of it she still might be."

It amused him he'd been involved with his current fling's mother. He was about to pour himself more wine, but his friend's reply stopped him. "Astrid's nothing like her mother. Somehow, she's discovered what we were involved with. It's only a matter of time before she finds out every detail. She and that accomplice of hers are out for revenge! I'd bear it in mind if I were you. Don't forget everything you've accomplished can be taken away from you at any time."

Not waiting for a response, Joel left the flat. The past was about to catch up with them and unlike his old friend he wasn't willing to keep a low profile. The girl wasn't a naive fool. They had too much to lose and his old friend's threat to expose him was a time bomb waiting to explode.

CHAPTER FIVE

THE DARK BEDSIT was empty except for some old paper boxes the bony figure had brought with him. Sitting on the dirty floor in a corner by the window, he had been crying for hours on end. Sobbing uncontrollably, thinking about the dead man who was dragged out of the river, he burst into laughter. "You deserved to die after what you did!"

It was close to midnight and without anything to eat or drink, he wondered when the girl would turn up.

Hours later, seated in the same corner, much too hungry and dehydrated to think straight, he got up from the floor, dragging his feet towards the filthy mattress by the small bathroom. Eyes closed and mouth dry at the memory of what happened years ago, he continued to cry. Soon everything he planned would come true. Eager to see and touch what reminded him of another place and time, he crawled towards one of the boxes, and pulled out a small black velvet box.

Hands shaking, opening the lid, he looked at the ring, turning it around to read the engraved letters on the inside. "For CX with gratitude for services rendered AL."

Elias Fleming, did you really imagine you'd get away with what you did? The girl's mistaken. Ingrid was too deep in for her own good. Did you put them up to it, saying she was a threat that had to be dealt with? I bet you took great pleasure in making her believe you cared for her. She was too fragile to save herself. Who killed you? Someone must have known about your shady past. You tried to escape the past and now you're dead.

Returning the ring to its box, he crawled back and lay down on the mattress. *I mustn't give up now. I'll have plenty of time to sleep in a bed when everything's over.* Looking up at the ceiling, light streaming in from the big window facing the common outside, he thanked his lucky stars the girl had suggested he squat in the derelict building overlooking Holst Enterprises across the common.

It had been child's play to access Joel Wranger's car. The girl found spare keys in the bottom drawer of his office desk and had them copied at the local hardware store. He'd soon figure out she wasn't working on her own.

With a wicked smile, he proceeded to take a trip down memory lane. Everything had been so easy back then. But that was a long time ago. Long before things started to go wrong, and everything he'd been dreaming of turned into a living hell.

It's our duty to expose the men who turned their backs on us. Daniel and Joel, you'll not escape so easily this time round.

* * * *

"What's up, honey?" Daniel asked suspiciously. The girl had gone out of her way to impress him in and out of bed. Joel was mistaken, she had nothing on him; no one did. Flashbacks from a different place and time made him queasy. Closing his mind to them, he repeated the question, eyes glued to her face. "What's up, honey? You look as if you've got something on your mind."

She replied, "You're wrong. Tonight's been great. Will you stay the night?"

"Nah, I've stayed the night too many times this week. Let's take it slowly; it's not as if we're married." He loved the confusion in her big blue eyes. If what Joel suspected of her was true, and she was out to pay him back for something he wasn't aware of, he'd find out about it from his friend sooner or later.

"Sure, but I was under the impression we had a mutual agreement to tell each other if things got out of hand... It's not my intention to nag you into staying the night if that's not what you want."

"Don't worry about it, honey. I'm a very busy man with many commitments. How about I take you out to dinner later this week? You get to choose the venue. Does that sound good to you?"

Astrid nodded. "I look forward to it. Thanks for coming by tonight. I enjoyed it very much."

"Good. I'll call you in a couple of days. Meanwhile, I want you to take a short break. You look as if you need some time to yourself." He enjoyed watching her squirm, concerned she'd perhaps not figured him out as well as she'd believed.

"Okay, since you're offering I wouldn't mind having some time off… I can't wait to see you again soon."

Standing next to her in her tiny kitchen, Daniel said, "I'll ask Joel to pick you up and drive you into town if that's what you want. A pretty young girl like you must be keen to visit department stores. I'll even give you some money right now to spend as you wish."

Her face turned pale, eyes frightened. He smiled at her. "Of course, I forgot you're not exactly his number one fan. Book a cab on me, tell whichever firm you use I'll foot the bill. All of them know I'm a very generous man." He omitted telling her numerous girlfriends had taken him up on his offers in the past.

"I'll be fine on my own. However safe most of them are, I don't want to take the risk. Goodbye, Daniel, I wish you a safe drive home."

She watched him pick up his car keys from the kitchen table and blow her a kiss on his way out the door. Then she proceeded to lock the front door and return to the kitchen. She'd pretended to be someone other than who she really was, despite keeping her real name. Her surname was common and she hadn't expected he'd put two and two together and figure out the truth just yet. All she wanted was some more time before he discovered what she and her accomplice had in store for him and his security man. *By the time you do, everything we've planned will be over and done with.*

CHAPTER SIX

"I WISH WE DIDN'T have to hide ourselves from them!" Astrid told her accomplice when she visited, bringing sandwiches and coffee she'd made after Daniel left her. They were in the hidden place evaluating recent events.

Face etched with pain, the sad figure of a human being rose from the floor. "Not yet. The time's not right. We've got a lot to do before that. Are you scared they'll try to stop us?"

"No, only concerned they'll discover what we have in store for them too soon. Daniel's been asking too many questions." She was close to tears, after suffering with flashbacks from the past and Daniel's consistent mentioning of the tablets in her bathroom cabinet. Clearly, they'd been preying on his mind ever since his first time in her flat.

The man put an arm around her and asked in a suspicious voice, "What kind of questions? We agreed you'd continue sleeping with him a while longer."

She knew if she ruined the plan she would never be forgiven. "Nothing in particular, just a few observations. He went through my bathroom cabinet and discovered the sleeping tablets and antidepressants. He asked why I take them."

The stranger screamed, "Ingrid would have been ashamed of you! She always trusted you to do what's expected of you! You must tell him you've ceased to take them since starting to work for him and that you only used them after a friend died. If they suspect you've been hiding something from them… It doesn't bear thinking of. Be careful when you're with Holst! If he suspects we're out to get revenge for his part in your poor mother's demise, game's over."

His pale blue eyes bored into hers, and she felt scared. Perhaps she had made a mistake getting involved with this person, but there was no going back now. "I wish we could stop now before it's too late."

"Don't be so stupid! We must continue what we've started." He pulled her close and whispered in her ear, "Everything will soon be over. You must stay patient until then. Ingrid would have been very proud of you."

The mention of her mother made Astrid's tears subside. "It's all I care about. I can't continue much longer… coming here when it's dark and continuing to be involved with that man." She bent to pick up her bag from the floor, eyes lingering on her accomplice one more time, before leaving.

* * * *

"We insist you cooperate with us, Mr. Holst!" said Morten Knudsen. "We've discovered the victim had a criminal record and was involved with drugs. Mr. Wranger owned up to knowing him. Make it easy on yourself and admit the three of you were part of gangs breaking into people's homes and much more in Bergen. We'll find out eventually so you may as well come clean now."

Livid that Joel had revealed they were acquainted with the dead man, Daniel hissed, "I won't admit to anything without my lawyer present!" So far he didn't know who Astrid's accomplice was but he feared his and Joel's lives might be in danger if what he suspected was true. They'd put their criminal past behind them and spent years regretting getting involved with the Bergen syndicate, participating in local burglaries, and leaving Ingrid behind. If he could go back, he knew he'd have brought her with him. The past they'd left behind years ago was finally catching up with them and there wasn't a thing either of them could do to change it.

CHAPTER SEVEN

THERE WAS NO doubt in Daniel's mind: Joel was a liability. The sooner he distanced himself from certain people the better. He just wished he knew how to do that after all the years he'd depended on Joel to get him out of tight spots.

"You're an idiot," he told Joel. "Can't you see what you've done? Thanks to your big mouth, you've compromised my high position! What possessed you? Things were going so well, the police would have left us alone if it weren't for you!" Reeling with anger, Daniel felt a migraine coming along.

Joel said, "They'd have discovered our part in what took place back then eventually. It was only a matter of time before they put two and two together. Bergen and Sandviken in particular are much too small for things to go unnoticed. Perhaps we ought to have foreseen it."

Increasingly agitated, Daniel shouted, "You mean you ought to have done something about it. All of it is down to your inability to do your job! The police have nothing on me. You on the other hand have quite a few skeletons in your past! If you imagine I'll cover your back, think again!" The prospect of ending up in prison over something he'd been involved with all those years ago made him nauseous.

Daniel hissed, "If that bastard blabbed about me to some idiot, implicating me in what happened and you've planted a seed of suspicion in that officer's head... For a start you'll lose your job and I'll make sure no one will give you a job ever again, is that clear? I demand you withdraw your statement immediately or you'll be out in the cold. See how far your 'credentials' will get you then!" He brushed past Joel on his way out and slammed the door.

Crushed he had no option but to abide by Daniel's wish and tell the police officer he'd been mistaken saying what he did, Joel sat down on a chair by the window overlooking the ugly building across the common.

His eyes fell on a window on the seventh floor, where someone was standing behind a dark curtain, flicking it aside to get a view of the surrounding properties and Daniel's luxurious premises. The ugly old building was being refurbished into a block of modern upmarket apartments. Most of the work was well underway, and the units were now being advertised to affluent people looking for places to invest in.

Joel thought the person behind the curtain must be a squatter who had broken into the building. He decided to check it out. Standing up to get a closer look, he saw a figure moving around inside the room. He reached for the binoculars on the top shelf, next to the office desk.

What met his eyes caused him to tremble all over. He'd been right to be concerned. His worst nightmare had come true. Breaking out in a cold sweat, he realized who Astrid's accomplice was. He'd suffered nightmares causing sleep deprivation since Knudsen had interrogated them about whether he and Daniel knew the dead man in the river.

Daniel has no idea what we're dealing with here... And the girl's too young and vengeful to believe we had nothing to do with what happened. I've got to do something before it's too late and more people end up the same way as Elias.

Turning on his mobile, Joel called the police station and asked to speak to Morten Knudsen.

"Mr. Wranger, what can I assist you with at this time of night? Perhaps you and your friend decided to come clean about your connection with the victim? If that's the case, I want you both here first thing in the morning. I'll be at my desk at seven a.m. Don't waste my time."

The smug voice made him tremble deep inside. "It's not the reason I called. I've got something to tell you. I noticed someone moving inside the building next door. I wouldn't have bothered to alert you if I wasn't convinced someone's living there. Squatters frequently break into derelict buildings. I think you ought to check it out." He hoped this might distract the officer and get him off his and Daniel's backs for the time being and give them enough time to figure out what to do next.

"You're sure about that? No one else has reported anyone in that building. We don't have funding for around the clock security checks, and Holst Enterprises turned down the borough's request to help guard empty properties in the area."

"I'm sorry about that but our security people have their hands full protecting our premises after last year's break-ins by local gangs. And yes, I'm sure or I wouldn't have called and wasted your time. Someone's living there. The place isn't exactly secure with builders coming and going as they please."

"Hmm, I'll make sure the borough looks into the matter." The police were pushed for time, their top priority the victim in the river. "Mr. Wranger, if it turns out you've wasted my time with some cock and bull story, to distract us from your and Mr. Holst's potential connection with the deceased man, you'll be very sorry indeed." Knudsen ended the call before Joel had the chance to say goodbye.

Standing in the darkness of the room, Joel sighed. *After all those years, the past's returned to haunt us. The girl's much too involved. We won't get her on our side.* Clenching his hands into fists, he didn't hold much hope. He prayed the person inside that building would be arrested. The Boss relied on Joel to keep him safe. Joel started to put together a plan. It was too late for regrets. Time was running out.

CHAPTER EIGHT

AFTER HER ACCOMPLICE texted Astrid and reported seeing someone watching him from the Holst building, she knew she had to find a new hiding place. She found a room in a nearby motel, off the beaten track.

The owner was an ex-convict she had known when they both lived in Sandviken years ago. He had relocated to Oslo after serving a prison sentence for armed robbery. He was now involved with a religious sect and accepted her plea for a place to hide, no questions asked...

She paid enough to cover two weeks until the job was completed. After he assured her of complete privacy, Astrid was satisfied her accomplice would be safe there. She wondered who had spotted him and was worried that whoever it was would report him to the police as a squatter.

When she returned to work later that day, after having a late lunch before her shift started, Joel approached her in the staff canteen on the ground floor, asking the reason she'd not showed up for work several days that week. She was afraid he'd been following her and seen who she visited, but she looked him in the eyes and said, "I don't answer to you! You've had it in for me from the start. Care to enlighten me of the reason?"

Joel glared at her and threw his hands up. "Daniel and I go back a long time. We're always there for each other. He focuses on the running of this place while I look after everything else. We're like brothers."

"What's that got to do with me?" she said. "Stop following me or I'll make sure Daniel knows about it. He knows how much I despise you. You make my skin crawl each time you come near me!"

He took a step away from her, and she heard him catch his breath. She was repulsed by his pale face and greasy brown hair. Joel Wranger was a creep, chasing underage girls. If it wasn't for Daniel giving him a job, he'd have no one giving a damn whether he lived or died.

Joel grabbed her right arm and held it in a firm grip. "You little whore! Did you imagine you could hide your friend from me? I saw him last night! If you continue to hide him from the police I'll report you to the police!"

Realizing Joel was behind her friend's relocation to another hiding place, Astrid composed herself, pretending she didn't care. "Be my guest. I've no idea what you're on about but I'll tell Daniel you're spying on me and making absurd accusations." Disentangling herself from his grip on her arm, she walked away.

In the bathroom, she splashed cold water on her face. She felt relieved she'd persuaded the motel owner to pick up and drive her friend to the new hiding place when it turned dark. Even if Joel reported him to the police, an officer probably wouldn't get to the empty building before then. Drained of emotions and exhausted due to sleep deprivation after what she and Daniel were up to when he'd stayed the night, she couldn't help feeling something wasn't right.

Her accomplice showered her with praise and affection yet withdrew each time she questioned him about what happened leading up to her mother's death. She'd been trying to find out the truth for so long she'd resorted to sleeping tablets and antidepressants to survive and live with the pain inside ever since losing her mother when she was ten.

Social services had placed her in a foster home close to where she'd lived with her mother, but no matter how nice and loving they were towards her, her foster parents weren't her real parents and were incapable of replacing her mother. She and Ingrid had shared a special bond. She missed her mother, and their next-door neighbors, Bodil and her daughter Aase. After Astrid had moved to her foster home, Bodil and Aase had dropped her and not visited her in her new home.

It wasn't until leaving the foster home when she turned sixteen that Astrid started to search for her father. After a few years of fruitless searching, with not a single trace of him, she'd cut her losses and made the decision to find the man she vividly recalled her mother was involved with when she was a little girl. The man who had meant a lot to her mother and left her to fend for herself and her child. She'd not had much luck finding out where he lived until she went through her mother's possessions in an old suitcase she'd been hiding in the closet in the room social services arranged in a nearby hostel. At sixteen she was too young to cope on her own with no inheritance to invest in a future home.

Reading the diary her mother left behind, Astrid discovered the man's name was Daniel Holst. He'd been a petty criminal whose shady past was erased when he left Bergen and started afresh in Oslo. Her mother was heartbroken when he disappeared from her life, referring to him as the man who made her the happiest yet also unhappiest she'd ever been.

Crying, feeling her mother's heartbreak, Astrid had concluded that Ingrid had been devastated when Daniel left her. Astrid thought it must have been he who destroyed her and her mother's lives. She believed Ingrid had committed suicide, shooting herself that night, and that somehow Daniel had driven her to it.

In the next few years Astrid survived on odd jobs, assisting in the local newsagent and waitressing in cafes and restaurants. At eighteen she was finally old enough to leave the hostel and rent a cheap bedsit not far from her old foster home. Getting by on what she made in cafes and restaurants, she applied for a secretarial position working part time in a local builder's office and continued working nightshifts to save up enough money to move to Oslo to get close to the man who had abandoned her and her mother.

She'd finally left Sandviken and rented a bedsit in Oslo, and soon after applied for a job in the accounts department at Holst Enterprises. Astrid had witnessed firsthand the strong bond between Daniel and Joel when seeing them together after she'd started working there. It was easy applying for a job since she'd obtained glowing references from everyone she'd worked for in Sandviken.

Her accomplice had contacted her out of the blue shortly after she'd moved to Oslo and started to work at Holst Enterprises. He told her he knew her mother years ago and found out where she lived from her and her mother's old neighbors. Despite the fact that they had never visited her, Astrid had called and informed them she was moving to Oslo in case they ever wanted to contact her.

Her accomplice was adamant that the two of them become good friends and insisted they get revenge on the man both believed had betrayed her mother.

Yet lately she'd been wondering why her accomplice hated Daniel so much. Whenever she asked about it, he refused to answer her, claiming everyone knew how badly The Boss had treated her mother. He'd made her believe Daniel and Joel were behind everything bad that had happened to Astrid as well.

After months of soul searching, she was in turmoil and started to wonder whether the man's accusations and wild assumptions were true or just lies to get her on his side. Something didn't add up. She had yet to discover what really happened the night her mother died.

Splashing more water on her face, she felt even worse than she had when informed of her mother's passing, once more wondering who her father was. *Please God, don't let it be Daniel. I couldn't live with myself if it turns out I've slept with my own father.* Sickened by the possibility, she cried for what seemed like an eternity, vowing to find out the truth about the night her mother died and her father's identity. Despite having mixed emotions about Daniel, she wasn't convinced he was responsible for what had happened to her mother.

Arriving at the small motel one hour later, scared she'd been seen entering the dark entrance and taking the lift upstairs to the third floor, she knocked on the door. Too frightened to think straight when no one answered, she pushed it wide open and entered the room.

The sight of a body lying in a pool of blood on the floor next to the bed made her scream so loud the owner rushed upstairs, taking in the ugly scene. White as a sheet in the face, he shouted, "What the hell's happened here? We've got to get rid of the body... I can't be connected with this... situation! The police monitor my every move, since my release from prison. I'm lucky they even gave me permission to run this place. Who's the dead man? Christ, he seemed weird, but I never imagined this! Who hated him so much they wanted him dead?"

Shaking her head, she replied, "Your guess is as good as mine. Unless... it's the only explanation. Joel Wranger's head of security at Holst Enterprises. After he discovered my friend's whereabouts he reported it to the police... He must have followed him to this place and killed him."

She'd been right all along. Daniel's right arm had gotten rid of the person who knew about their past in Bergen.

"Joel shot him? No, no, no! He and I go back a long time. We went to school together in Bergen. He was here earlier today, asking about your friend, accusing me of hiding him. I told him he was mistaken, that I'd never get involved with shady people after what I went through. Joel said you work for

The Boss, and that you and the dead man were planning revenge on the two of them over some misunderstanding years ago. I told him I'd stay in touch if something bad happened.

"After Joel left, I checked your friend. I brought him a bottle of red wine and toasted cheese sandwiches he'd ordered earlier. He seemed fine, thanked me for letting him stay here, and said you'd be joining him later. The killer must have used the back entrance while I was downstairs tending to guests and bookings in the last couple of hours."

He told her he distinctly recalled that he'd seen the man alive well after Joel had left. "What will you do now? I refuse to get more involved than I already am."

Astrid replied, "I understand. Please help me clean up and transport the body to my flat. I've rented a car; it's outside in the parking lot."

"Alright, but that's all I'm willing to do. Sooner or later you have to tell the police; you can't hide him forever or your place will smell."

"Thanks, I know, but what will I tell them? That I hid the body because I was scared to report it? They'll arrest me and charge me with murder," she cried. The stranger's plan was the only thing that had kept her sane, now that he was dead everything they'd planned, getting revenge on Daniel and Joel by threatening to expose their past, would never happen.

"I wish I never became involved with this… this insanity! But I was so sure he knew the truth, and I put my trust in that man! Please just do as I ask. Daniel owes me an explanation of what took place all those years ago! You must call Joel and make sure he helps get rid of the body. Tell him we'll report his visit here to the police if he doesn't help."

Half an hour later, Joel arrived and helped the owner carry the body wrapped in a sheet downstairs to his old station wagon in the parking lot.

They decided the owner would return Astrid's rented car and clean up traces of blood and fingerprints in the room later, and Joel would drive her home. Watching him and the motel owner carry the body down to the river where the other body had been discovered, then throw it into the water, she felt nauseous, thinking the killer might come after her next.

Returning to the car minutes later, Joel thanked the other man for helping them. "I give you my word no one will ever know about it. Make sure you clean up every trace of him. Sooner or later his body will be discovered and the police will start asking questions."

"You know me; I'll make sure they won't find anything that incriminates us. We should keep a low profile and not be in touch until the killer's been found and arrested."

Shaking his head, Joel replied, "I'm not taking any chances; we're better off not being in touch at all. At least now we know the dead man's no longer capable of taking revenge on me and Daniel for something that's not our fault."

Shaking hands, the motel owner got out of the car and walked back to the motel.

Too distraught to talk, Astrid didn't say a word during the drive back to her flat.

After dumping the body in the river, Joel thought about the dead man. His name was Cory Xander, a former pimp and drug dealer in Bergen who knew Elias Fleming and had dated Ingrid a few times before she became involved with Daniel. Joel was pleased he was no longer a threat to either of them. All he had to do now was convince the girl her father was a very bad man, whom her mother had been scared of. He prayed after tonight she'd stop hating him and Daniel.

Dropping her off outside her flat, informing her he was there for her if she needed him, he watched her unlock the front door and get inside. It wasn't until he'd parked his car in the garage and gone upstairs to his flat that the realization of what lay in store for them hit him like a sledge hammer. Whoever had killed Elias and Cory might be coming after him and Daniel. After all, they'd all been part of the same crime syndicate all those years ago.

CHAPTER NINE

"HOW SURE ARE you that man's body won't be traced to us?" Daniel asked Joel the following morning.

"Only as sure as I can be. I think Elias and Cory were killed by the same person. They'll be coming after us next. To them we're a liability they can't ignore, seeing as we were involved with very dubious people in Bergen. I wish there was something I could do to protect us, but the situation is out of my control."

Daniel stared at him in disbelief. "We've always known the past might catch up with us one day. Everything we've accomplished counts for nothing unless we can come up with a plan, anything to put a stop to this insane fixation with us and what happened in another lifetime! Or are you suggesting we accept the inevitable and end up like those men? I always knew Ingrid wouldn't last much longer. Not after all the affairs with men who exploited her kindness and naive belief they truly cared for her. My warnings fell on deaf ears after we broke up. We continued to stay in touch until *he* appeared in her life. I hardly saw her after that until that fateful night. Do you recall how much she pleaded with me to return to her? She was terrified of her lover, even at times scared he'd harm her and her little girl. I'll never forget the desperation in her eyes when I told her I was leaving and starting a new life." His voice faltered at the memory of how much she once meant to him.

"Yeah, I remember everything like it was yesterday. All the petty crimes we got ourselves involved with to earn enough to escape our families. I know I'll always feel guilty for robbing innocent people and mixing with criminals. But we've paid for our mistakes and don't deserve to die. Astrid's desperate to find her father. You're absolutely certain it's not you?"

Daniel whispered, "One hundred percent. You're aware I had an irreversible vasectomy when I was twenty years old. Astrid and I are lovers. I'd hardly have slept with my own daughter! Anyway, she was born after I ended my affair with her mother."

Looking down at his hands, he recalled how much Ingrid had relied on him always being there for her, and he was reminded of his own despair and horrible parents. The product of an abusive relationship, and the only child of a former prostitute and an alcoholic, Daniel had been the victim of abuse, beaten by his father since he was a young child. His mother always turned a blind eye, blaming him for everything that went wrong in her life.

He'd run away from home several times, fending for himself and finding shelter with street gangs tempting him to get involved with crimes to make enough money to leave the dreary neighborhood and move to Oslo.

He'd worked so hard to put everyone and everything behind him and rebuild his life and existence. No one was permitted to enter that new life except Joel, who knew the real reason behind his determination to succeed no matter at what cost.

It took years to be where he was now, and much longer coming to terms with the past, dealing with what his parents had put him through when they ought to have loved and protected their only child.

Daniel survived on odd jobs for new friends in Oslo when he first arrived. It didn't take long before he was offered full-time positions in small successful businesses where he'd been responsible for customer relations and incorporation of new ideas, beating the competition. Rumor soon had it he was a force to be reckoned with and as the years went by, Daniel accumulated a vast network of Oslo's and Scandinavia's elite contacts, furthering his success and eventually the opportunity to start his own business.

Holst Enterprises quickly achieved much success and was the company to deal with in everything from leisure to real estate and luxurious retreats and holidays. Everything Daniel was involved with turned into more successes and the financial security he always wanted since he was a young boy in Bergen.

Joel put a hand on Daniel's shoulder. "I know how hard you've worked to be successful and achieve everything you've got, the hotels, restaurants and real estate. We're miles apart, you and me, yet we share a special bond after everything we've endured. Please listen to me. We've got to do something to prevent another tragedy! I don't know what to do… We've got to face this thing or risk losing everything we've accomplished."

Nodding, Daniel embraced him, saying, "I agree, tell me everything you know."

Joel replied, "Astrid's father's the key to all of it… Ingrid had an especially destructive relationship with one man in particular. Astrid's idolized her mother for so long she won't accept her failings. Ingrid was depressed, relying on men to provide for her and Astrid and protect them. Instead she got involved with the wrong people, who used her for their own purposes. You must end your fling with her daughter. Let her go, Daniel."

To Joel's surprise, his old friend nodded. "You're right. Astrid's a lovely girl but I decided a long time ago to not get emotionally involved with anyone. Ever since I discovered she's Ingrid's daughter, I've been feeling sorry for her and ashamed of what we've done. You're the only person who knows how much her mother meant to me. I don't want to go through the same pain again. I get the impression you know the identity of the man Ingrid was so scared of. She never mentioned his name to me and refused to introduce me to him."

Looking his old friend in the eyes, Joel replied, "You're right, I think I do. Please trust me on this and don't ask any questions."

Leaving him standing there, too confused to speak and attempting to figure out who it might be, Joel returned to his flat and packed a suitcase, wishing his friend could have come with him. This was his responsibility, and he knew only too well if he failed, he'd bring everyone down with him.

CHAPTER TEN

ASTRID FELT BEREFT. "Why are you ending things between us, what have I done to deserve it?" She wasn't in love with him but had grown to like him, which was the last thing she'd expected. Ever since he and Joel had revealed their true colors, being there for her and making sure she wasn't alone in the flat, both men made her feel safe and cared for.

She and Daniel were in her bedroom when he told her they weren't together for the right reasons and ought to end their affair. Reaching for her hand, he pulled her close to him, replying "You've got a lot to deal with at such a young age. The reason I left Bergen all those years ago was because I had to get away from there and rebuild my life.

"I'm not the same scared, immature young man I was then, escaping a violent alcoholic father and mother who didn't give a damn about me. Everything I've accomplished was down to me and all the hard work I put in to get to where I am now.

But I was a fool, imagining I'd come to terms with the past. Some things stay with you indefinitely. You haven't had the opportunity to reconcile with what happened to your mother. Joel's traveling to Sandviken to find the answers we require to move on."

The three of them were different people now, desperate to get closure and leave the past behind once and for all. "You and I weren't meant to be, honey, but I do care for you. From now on I'll take care of your bills. You're doing a great job and are welcome to continue working for me if that's what you want."

"I don't know what to say. I'm sorry I lied to you about who I am and the reason I applied for a job in accounts. That man... Sometimes I felt Mor put him before me. I was too young to understand how miserable and depressed she was. But deep down I know how much she loved me, and she was good to me. Did you really care for her?"

Her eyes welled up with tears. She'd hated him for so long only to discover he wasn't the cause of her mother's unhappiness. Listening to him, she believed him when he said he'd cared for her mother. Unlike the man who was her father and made her mother feel scared and unhappy.

"Very much, but I was young and had a lot to deal with. If I could go back I'd have handled things differently. Hindsight is a wonderful thing. I've spent years pretending to be someone who doesn't care. I don't want to do that anymore and neither should you. Don't make the same mistakes I did. You must find inner peace and the strength to move on."

Listening to him, Astrid suddenly felt agitated, knowing firsthand how hard it was to reconcile with the past. "I know you're right but looking back, I feel so upset Mor was too fragile and damaged to make the right choices. I can hardly recall her voice. Joel won't be able to change what happened. We're better off trying to forget about it. I'll never know who my father is. I've spent too much time wondering and probably always will." She cried, tears spilling down her face and neck.

Kissing her cheek, Daniel gently withdrew from her, saying, "I disagree. I feel certain he wants to know you and be part of your life. There's a reason he's not been looking for you."

Acutely conscious of the intimacy they'd been sharing, she asked, "Do you suppose you and Mor might have worked out if you hadn't left and she hadn't gotten involved with my father?"

"Maybe. Honestly, I don't know the answer. But this I know for sure: Ingrid would have been very proud of you and how well you've coped despite the awful circumstances surrounding her death." His eyes turned sad just thinking about what might have been.

They continued to talk a while longer, and then he left her and returned home.

* * * *

"You owe me!" Joel shouted into his cell phone. "I've no doubt you're destitute and need money. I'll ask you again: Where is he hiding and does he use another name? Tell me and I'll give you some money and never bother you again."

He was in a hotel room a few blocks from the old neighborhood in Sandviken, having arrived late the previous night. He hadn't bothered with breakfast, just several mugs of steaming hot black coffee to keep him awake after a sleepless night.

His mother's high-pitched voice made him nauseous, reminding him of all the times it haunted him in his nightmares. "What makes you so sure I have the answers you need? Your idiot brother left years ago, and I haven't heard from him in a long time."

Anger threatening to suffocate him, he lost his temper. "You've no right to live after everything you and Dad put me through! I'm glad he's dead; at least now he won't destroy other people's lives anymore! You have no idea how hard I've tried to overcome what he did to me… molesting his own sons! I even went to prison after being convicted of sleeping with underage girls! Can you imagine how I felt after everything I endured?"

He instantly regretted revealing too much. He'd found a good therapist and after much soul searching came to terms with what had led him to get involved with minors. Unlike his father, he had dealt with his problems.

"You went to prison? You're your father's son, alright! I wish it was your brother calling me instead of you! The least you can do is give your old mum money to keep a roof over my head."

"I owe you nothing! Since you're refusing to help me, I hope you rot in hell! I'll find my brother without you."

He ended the call, convinced she had the answers he needed. If what he believed was true, the truth would come out eventually. Meanwhile, a killer was on the loose, possibly planning the next installment of his devious plan. Joel wasn't prepared to ignore his gut instinct; he had done that too many times and lived to regret it.

Chapter Eleven

SANDVIKEN. AKSEL HAD forgotten how beautiful it was, pushing to the back of his mind that fatal night and vowing to not return and dig up the past he'd so desperately tried to bury. He'd kept a low profile since being discharged from the psychiatric hospital where he'd been incarcerated on and off for nearly ten years and confined to a solitary room while he ingested a cocktail of medical drugs.

When he left, the psychiatrist made him promise to return for regular checkups, but instead of keeping his promise, he'd managed to get hold of the key to the medicine cabinet and stolen enough tranquilizers and antidepressants to maintain the calmness he so desperately needed to execute his revenge on the people he held responsible for what was wrong in his life. He'd endured a hellish childhood, with consistent abuse and consequently mistrusted people around him.

He'd been sufficiently good-looking to attract women but they reminded him of his mother, the same vulgar appearance and cheap behavior. Increasingly reliant on drugs to help him cope on a daily basis, he'd been diagnosed with psychopathic tendencies and paranoia. In his mind, everyone was out to get him and consequently an enemy.

After repeated attempts to kill himself with sleeping tablets and harm himself with sharp objects, he'd concluded his life was merely an existence, and being confined to a mental hospital from time to time was his destiny. That was okay with him, as long as he was able to call the shots and work towards getting revenge on the people who had betrayed him.

Out of the blue, he'd bumped into Elias Fleming one late evening in Sandviken, after he'd revisited his old house, spying on the old haggard woman who was his mother. Too upset to think straight, he'd had dinner in a newly opened restaurant nearby, instantly recognizing the man who used to work for the same syndicate years ago.

Pretending they weren't acquainted, Elias was about to leave when Aksel stopped him and persuaded him to have a drink and talk about the old days. After that night they'd kept in touch sporadically. It had been easy to trick Elias into meeting him again in Oslo, saying he wanted to remunerate him for offering him the chance to take part in a burglary in the capital's premier jewelry store. He told Elias the bar on the common by the river would be a safer place to hand over the money rather than outside where they'd be in full view of people passing by.

During the periods between hospitalizations, Aksel had taken odd jobs in sleazy wine bars and motels in bad areas of Bergen and Oslo and done odd jobs for drug barons and anyone else paying well for his services. He'd managed to cope on antidepressants and tranquilizers, and when they ran out, his acquaintances gave him similar drugs.

What Elias Fleming didn't know was that his friendship with Holst and Wranger would cost him his life. Aksel had spiked Elias' drink with Rohypnol, and when Elias began to feel drowsy, offered to drive him back to his motel... Elias had fallen into a deep drunken coma, unaware he'd never see daylight again.

It was child's play carrying the body into the deepest part of the river and watching it sink.

Weeks later, he'd discovered Cory Xander's hiding place in a derelict building not far from there, and put two and two together when seeing him with some girl from his hiding place in a small shed nearby...

My daughter cared more about that creep than me, her own father. It irked him knowing she'd put her faith in a complete stranger whose only wish was to take revenge on Holst and Wranger for tricking him out of his share from a burglary the three of them had committed together years earlier in a wealthy private home in Bergen.

Ever since then, Cory Xander had hated them and told everyone he knew about Daniel's affair with Ingrid. What better way for Xander to get revenge on Daniel than through Ingrid's daughter?

Aksel had followed her to that motel, and after she left, he returned and tricked the owner into giving him a spare key to the back entrance, buying his sob story of how much he'd missed his long lost uncle and wanted to surprise him.

The owner even offered him a room free of charge, and a bottle of red wine and ham sandwiches with melted cheese. He bribed the man to keep his mouth shut in case someone saw him entering Xander's room. An ex-convict with a track record of violent behavior, he readily agreed to not breathe a word to anyone.

Xander never knew what happened until it was too late. He was sitting on the edge of the bed when Aksel came up behind him. One shot in the head and he was gone... The owner must have figured out who did it yet kept his promise to keep quiet.

The girl and Wranger must have disposed of Xander's body in the river just like Aksel had done with Fleming's body.

With the murders only a few weeks apart, the police were bound to become suspicious and link the two victims, thinking the same killer was behind both. The time had arrived to set in motion the next installment of his plan and rid himself of the men who stood in his way and knew too much. The girl was an unexpected bonus he couldn't wait to get rid of as well. *My daughter doesn't give a damn about me. She deserves to die.*

It wasn't until much later he realized he'd made a mistake. He'd not remembered it until now. *I forgot to bring with me the rings I pulled off Elias and Xander's fingers... They were made for them by the person Ingrid became involved with after she ended our relationship...*

Praying the police didn't find them when searching for evidence, he started to lighten up and smiled, convincing himself he had nothing to worry about. No one knew about him, he'd been in hiding for so long he'd almost forgotten his own identity and reason he wanted to kill again. *Joel's getting much too close. He's trying to find out where I live. She told me when she called me out of the blue. It won't be long before he discovers where I am... the interfering bastard! Where was he when I needed him the most? Nowhere! I've got to kill him before the others! When he's close to dying he'll regret abandoning me and interfering in my life.*

CHAPTER TWELVE

MORTEN KNUDSEN WAS in a good mood following the interrogation of Holst and Wranger about their connection with Elias Fleming. One of his officers had discovered a ring with two sets of initials engraved on the inside. One set belonged to the victim, EF for Elias Fleming. The other set matched the name of one of the victims in a fatal double shooting in Sandviken ten years earlier.

There was something familiar in both cases. Knudsen distinctly recalled a similar scenario in the earlier case... A ring had been found in a house in Sandviken where two officers arrived after a neighbor reported hearing gunshots. Two people, a male and a female, were discovered inside, both shot in the back of the head. The ring found on the living room floor next to the male victim was identical to those found on the Oslo common after Fleming and Xander's bodies were found. It was this earlier male victim's initials that had been engraved inside all three rings.

Knudsen called the Sandviken police department and was informed the officer on that case had retired from the force five years ago. The case had not been reassigned and was never solved.

He asked to have the case reassigned to him, and ten minutes later, the case file appeared in his inbox. After reading the notes he whistled. "I'll be damned. Holst and Wranger knew all victims…"

Daniel Holst and his head of security were seriously at risk of being next in line to be executed. Knudsen's gut instinct told him it was just a matter of time. Driving home from work later that night, he suddenly realized the girl was in serious danger too. Astrid Jensen was the female victim's daughter. They had sufficient proof to link the cases and knew about the girl's connection with Xander but had yet to discover the reason.

He contacted the officer in charge of security to send out more men to her home. "We're not taking any risks until the killer's been found and arrested."

He was increasingly concerned; something didn't sit right with him. No matter how hard he tried, he wasn't capable of figuring out what it was yet.

CHAPTER THIRTEEN

"YOU CAN'T BE SERIOUS! Why do you think some lunatic wants me dead?" Too shocked to make sense of the young officer's announcement, Astrid watched him pull out a chair to sit across from her at the kitchen table.

"I've no details yet except your safety's our top priority from now on," he said. "Officers will be guarding you wherever you are. Apparently, we've sufficient reason to suspect someone's planning to kill you."

"But why me? You must tell me everything you know! How else will I be able to protect myself in case the killer knows where I live and turns up when you're not around?" She was fed up with living in constant fear.

"Someone will be with you all the time. Apparently, the killer knows who you are. The recent killings are connected with an old case in Sandviken, the suburb you and your mother used to live in outside Bergen… We're informed your father's coming after you. That's all I know."

Numb with fear, Astrid put a hand on her mouth, shaking her head. "No. That can't be true. I'm not sure who my father is. Mor was involved with different men…Why would he want me dead?"

Putting an arm around her shoulders, the officer attempted to calm her down. At this rate she was close to having a nervous breakdown. "You've had a nasty shock after everything you've been through lately," he said in a soothing voice.

Burying her face in her hands, she cried, "My own father wants to kill me! What have I ever done to make him hate me so much?" Sobbing uncontrollably, tears blurring her vision, she heard him say, "It isn't down to you, love. Clearly, he's not right in the head. We'll be watching over you. Let's get you into bed. You'll feel better later."

"Okay. But please don't leave me for a second! Thanks for being so nice to me," she said, thinking she must find out her father's identity and reason he wanted to kill her. He must have been the one who killed Cory.

The officer brought her coffee and toasted sandwiches in the morning before his colleague arrived to take over. "I'll return tonight. Try to stay calm; we're not letting you out of our sight."

Later that day, praying she'd be safe in her own home and wherever she went, Astrid held on to the hope the police were mistaken. *Surely, my own father doesn't hate me so much he wants to harm me.* Mor had been frightened of a man she didn't want Astrid to get to know. It was the reason she'd left Astrid with Bodil, the next-door neighbor, to keep him from seeing her. She was the happiest and yet also most scared whenever he visited. Cory had told her he knew the man. But what did that have to do with Daniel? And why did Cory hate him and Joel so much? She must find out the truth about her mother's death.

If only she was able to visit Sandviken and her mother's grave, perhaps then she'd get the answers she so desperately needed. She vividly recalled another of her mother's lovers, a young man who had made her mother so happy shortly before she'd died. He'd been her lover and was at least ten years younger than her. Mor had been involved with him while dating Astrid's father.

The man Mor hid her from must have been her father. Why else would she keep them apart? Astrid had not seen him often, but she suddenly remembered him now and the ugly scar on his left cheek. Mor said he'd been injured when he was very young. She said his father used to make him do things against his will and burned his cheek with a cigarette and that he'd never recovered from the abuse.

Each time he visited, her mother locked her inside her bedroom if the next door neighbor wasn't home. Once she'd been on her own when her mother was shopping, and he had entered through the unlocked front door. She was terrified, but he had only stared at her and then left without saying a word. When her mother found out about it, she'd made sure Astrid was never left on her own again and had changed the locks in case he had a key.

I wonder why I forgot about him. Mor made me think he was no one special. I must have suppressed the memory of him. I'll never forget that scar again. Mor must have known he was deranged. It must have incensed him to find out she was involved with another man. Someone told him about me and put my life at risk. For some reason he thinks I don't care about him.

If she was right, he wouldn't give up until he found her and executed his wish. Her life would be over unless she found him first. *What if he's here, in Oslo? He's waited a long time to meet me and kill me. That man who was found next to my mother... if only I could recall his name... I've got to return to Bergen and talk to Bodil. She lived next door and used to be Mor's friend and confidante. Surely she knew the names of both men.* She hoped the police wouldn't stand in her way.

CHAPTER FOURTEEN

DANIEL AND JOEL had been summoned to Knudsen's cramped office at the police station to be questioned once more about every move they had made on the night Ingrid and her lover were killed. Knudsen told them he was now in charge of both cases. "We've found the rings belonging to the victims. They're identical with the male victim's in Sandviken, and second set of initials engraved in all of them matched his name. Only the female victim didn't have a ring pulled off her long finger. The initials belonged to the man who was murdered in her home and lying next to her."

Daniel and Joel told Knudsen that Ingrid had invited them to dinner at her home that fatal night, and that they'd arrived at her home at eight o'clock and were joined by another guest.

"He was in his mid-twenties; I can't recall his name," Daniel said.

"He was younger than her. They were lovers and all over each other," Joel added.

"I see, well, I'll be visiting both of you individually to ask more questions later today." Knudsen gestured at the door, dismissing them for now, saying he was too busy to continue the interrogation there and then. He'd followed police procedure questioning them individually the first time and wanted to make sure they stood by their initial statements.

True to his word, Knudsen arrived at Daniel's flat later that day. Leading the way into the large kitchen, overlooking the panoramic views of the river outside, Daniel asked, "Would you like something to eat? I was just about to have lunch at the bar." He'd not slept a wink in the last week, painfully aware a killer was on the loose.

"I wouldn't mind some coffee and whatever you're having while we talk."

He sat on a high stool at the bar, and Daniel brought him a steaming hot mug of coffee and a cheese sandwich. He locked eyes with Daniel and asked, "How come Ingrid and that young man were an item?"

"I've no idea. They must have been in love; she and I were only together for a very short time."

"I see. Her daughter told me she liked him, and that he was always nice to her. She also said her mother kept her away from some man that used to visit from time to time." Knudsen was about to say something else when Joel entered the kitchen, looking angry.

"I called the station and was informed you're here. How come you didn't call and tell me you've been delayed? I was expecting you'd show up sooner." Standing at the bar, exchanging a worried look with his friend, he poured himself a mug of black coffee.

Ignoring him, the officer proceeded to talk. "I'm pleased you're here. It'll save me time to interrogate you together. I was about to reveal the male victim's name in Sandviken. The details were discovered in the initial report at the time."

"What was his name, officer?" Daniel asked in a low voice, knowing the answer before the officer gave it to them. "Andras Lyng. Judging by your facial expressions, it seems you knew him?"

"Perhaps the name rings a bell but I can't recall any details," Daniel replied, averting his eyes.

"Me neither," said Joel. "All I know is that he and Ingrid were an item for a short period of time, officer."

"I understand. Well, I bet this will surprise you, or maybe not. Andras Lyng worked in a large famous jeweler's in Bergen, specializing in custom-made jewelry. Lyng's expertise was designing and making customized rings. The rings belonging to the male victims were specially made by him."

Face drained of color, Joel whispered, "But that can't be right! I'd have known about it… Elias and I knew each other; he'd have mentioned it to me. I'm going to be straight with you, since you already know I went to prison for sleeping with underage girls. Daniel's been very good to me, standing by me and giving me a job. Andras Lyng used to be a member of the same syndicate as the one we were members of a long time ago. He took part in petty crimes but unlike us got himself involved with much bigger and more dangerous things. Daniel and I left Bergen and started a new life."

Livid his friend had revealed too much, Daniel put his hands up, saying, "I've built everything from scratch, officer. Despite what my parents did to me, I've survived and achieved everything I set out to do."

Ignoring him, Knudsen got up from his chair and walked to the window, turning to look at them. "Sure. I've no problem with that except both of you ought to have come clean about knowing the victims from the start instead of wasting our time. My time. We're aware of your past and association with Elias Fleming. He got himself involved with hardened criminals. We've got sufficient proof he was a pimp.

"Lyng wasn't as innocent as you may have believed at the time. He was involved with very dangerous people as well. He, Elias Fleming, and Corey Xander smuggled fake jewelry all over Scandinavia. Those rings were remuneration for a job well done and a trademark to get them noticed by organized high end jewelers using the pieces as cover for much more lucrative dealings: distribution of heroin in and outside of Norway, selling directly to other syndicates who were connected with international drug barons.

"When word got out they'd been using fake jewelry to camouflage their dealings, several syndicates fell out with each other and as a direct outcome, people involved with them didn't receive their share of the money. The ones losing out big time suspected their old mates had stolen what belonged to them. And when some of them sold out their fellow criminals to the police, they became victims of the killer whose life depended on the earnings of their criminal involvements. In some ways the two of you built your success from criminal offenses and other people's misfortunes."

Angry, he'd been accused of something he wasn't guilty of, Daniel said, "We got ourselves involved with the wrong people, officer, but we've never exploited anyone! How dare you stand there, accusing me of theft? You're mistaken; someone wants it to look that way. It's the reason we've opened up about our past and involvement with those people. You've no evidence of wrongdoing where we're concerned and you never will!"

Knudsen smiled at Daniel. "Care to enlighten me how a dirt poor small town crook like yourself made it so big? And please don't insult me, saying you worked your ass off! Everyone knows it didn't you take long to get to where you are now."

Daniel was close to hitting him in the face, but Joel positioned himself between them. "Can't you see? The police will never let us forget our past," he said to Daniel. "We were involved with the wrong people back then and still carry the burden of it. You used to be the poor kid that got beaten up by your parents and I'm the kid whose father molested young kids! No one gives people like us the benefit of doubt. No matter how much we've moved on, all the successes in the world won't erase how we used to be then."

He turned to Knudsen. "Listen to me, officer. We've not done anything wrong since leaving our homes behind. Sure, I picked up Elias' ring to take a closer look... How was I to know I was tampering with evidence and that some deranged killer was on the loose planning to kill again? Daniel and I paid for our mistakes."

Nodding, Knudsen took a step back. "I know neither of you are murderers. Yet someone out there hates you so much they want to kill you for something they believe is your fault and happened years ago. So far, we believe it was they who executed Astrid's mother, Lyng, Fleming, and Xander. All except Ingrid were involved with crimes. We reckon she was killed after witnessing her lover's murder. I've arranged round the clock protection for both of you and the girl. We've reason to believe all of you are the killer's next intended victims."

Shaking, Daniel asked in a trembling voice, "What's the plan, what will you do to stop it? Clearly, you've no idea who they are. That lunatic could be anywhere or here, in Oslo, as we speak! And what about Astrid? Are you sure she's guarded day and night?"

"I can assure you she's safe. From tonight both of you will get the same protection. One more thing: We've reason to believe the girl's the primary target since she's the female victim's daughter. You must dig deep into your minds and try to remember more details and when you do I'll be available at the usual number. Time's not on our side. I'll be in touch soon."

After he left, Joel said, "We've got to do what he asked. The killer's out to get us, one after the other. In the meantime, I'll try to come up with a solution to save our lives before it's too late.

CHAPTER FIFTEEN

"I CAN'T CONTINUE like this, with officers guarding me all the time everywhere I am! My father's coming after me and I've no idea why he hates me," Astrid cried as soon as Joel and Daniel came round to see how she was. She knew she looked tired and pale, and she felt awful they'd see her like that.

"Let's have lunch together in a restaurant," Daniel suggested. "What's your favorite food, Norwegian or perhaps Italian? I know this lovely quaint place on the outskirts of town that serves the best linguini I've ever tasted."

She shrugged and thanked him for being so kind to her. "This has never happened to me before; no one's ever threatened my life."

"Well, I guess there's always a first time for everything but you're not on your own in this," said Joel. "We're just as upset, but we won't permit some lunatic to dictate our lives. You'd do well to follow our example."

Daniel seated himself next to her on the couch in the far corner of the kitchen. "You must try to keep it together. Soon, all of it will become a distant memory. The police are on top of things. Can you remember something that might lead to an arrest? You told the officer in charge of the cases Ingrid was dating someone who caused her much pain yet made her happy. Any detail, however insignificant at the time, might help. I understand you were very young back then, yet this guy petrified your mother sufficiently for her to leave you with a neighbor each time she worried he'd come round."

Staring into space, willing herself to remember something, no matter how insignificant, she replied "I can't! I was ten years old and just a kid. The only thing I know is how scared Mor was of him, despite still caring for him. I recall the ugly scar on his face but if I remember too much and inform the police, he'll come after me and kill me and I'll end up like my mother. I can't risk it, please don't make me!" She was frantic the man she'd briefly seen all those years ago would find her and kill all of them, just like he did to the other people. It all brought back memories of finding out her mother had died.

Holding her hand in his, Daniel said, "No one will hurt you when I'm with you, but no matter how hard, you must try to remember details about him. How else will we be able to prevent what he's got in store for us?"

Nodding, Joel added, "You know he's got a point. Facing up to what scares us most is preferable to bottling things up."

Reflecting on what they told her, Astrid ran to the window and looked out on the street and pavement, recognizing the officer guarding her that afternoon. Turning to look at them, she asked, "Will you give me your word what I'm about to tell stays between ourselves?"

Exchanging worried looks, both men shook their heads.

Daniel said, "That depends on what you've got to tell us, honey. The police must be able to protect you. If we withhold vital information from them, they can't do that. Just tell us what you know and we'll decide whether to keep it between ourselves or not."

Feeling increasingly anxious they'd tell the police yet more scared if she didn't come clean about what she'd remembered, she whispered, "Mor told me my father said he'd hurt us if she didn't let him see me. At the time I couldn't make sense of what she told me. A couple of years later, I must have been twelve years old, after she died, I bumped into an old school friend. She asked what became of Mor's ex-boyfriend, Aksel. I told her I had no idea. She accused me of lying. It didn't make sense until recently."

Walking to the kitchen sink, she turned on the cold water tap, poured herself a glass of water, and drank it. Her old friend's comment was preying on her mind.

Daniel asked in a tense voice, "What else did she tell you, honey?"

Turning to face them, she replied, "She told me Mor confided in her mother that her new boyfriend, Andras, had received several threats over some deal he'd been part of and kept someone's share of the profit... Can't you see? He must have confided it to my mother, making her an accessory in the killer's mind. I bet it's the reason both were shot."

Joel said, "Are you suggesting Ingrid was witness to her boyfriend's murder and had to be silenced? But if that was the case, the police must have known he'd been killed first."

Sobbing, the girl shook her head. "I don't know but it seems that way. Please say you won't tell the police! If my father finds out I've figured out he killed them, he'll do whatever it takes to find out where I live, unless he already knows..."

They promised to keep secret what she had told them for a while longer.

"Let's get you to bed," said Joel. "You're looking ill and need to sleep."

Holding her on either side, they helped her into the bedroom, watched her fall into a restless sleep, and left.

Outside the flat, Daniel approached an officer outside the front door of the building and requested they not let her out of their sight. "You mustn't let on you know what I'm about to tell you. She made us promise we'd keep it to ourselves. Astrid just confided in us she found out her mother knew her boyfriend had received threats from someone claiming he stole their share from some break-in. She thinks her mother was killed because she witnessed his murder."

Promising to share the information with Knudsen, the officer said he'd make sure the girl never found out about it.

Driving back to work, Joel informed Daniel he needed some time off. "Don't ask me why. Just trust me when I tell you I know what I'm doing."

Too tired and exasperated to protest, Daniel did what he asked and got out of the car.

His friend, still inside, seemed lost in his own thoughts, saying out loud what Daniel had been dreading the most: "This time you'll pay for what you've done."

CHAPTER SIXTEEN

"YOU'RE LEAVING AND traveling to Bergen again? I thought we agreed you'd stay here." Furious his right arm and friend wouldn't tell him the reason, Daniel gestured at the cozy surroundings of the flat he'd bought for Joel when he became successful. "This is how you repay me, by traveling to Bergen of all places? I thought you got the answers you needed last time despite keeping it to yourself."

Throwing things into a suitcase, Joel replied, "I've been mistaken about a few things. It's the reason I have to revisit the old haunts. I'll be back soon."

"What am I supposed to do while you're away? Astrid's out of her mind worrying she'll be attacked in her own home, and I'm getting increasingly concerned we're next in line to be killed. It might happen when we least expect it. The police are useless, expecting us to stay calm! You're my head of security. I trust you with our lives, damn it!"

Daniel hadn't bothered to shave in the last few days. He was wearing torn, faded blue jeans and a white t-shirt. He hadn't had a wink of sleep for nights on end, fearing he'd be dead soon.

"Sit tight and watch your back. Astrid's safe with those officers guarding her twenty-four seven. Business is booming so no need to concern yourself with that. I'll be in touch as soon as I can." Putting a hand on his friend's back, saying goodbye, Joel carried his suitcase outside to the lift and stepped inside, pushing the button taking him to the garage where he'd parked his car. He had plenty of time to figure out his next move while driving to Bergen.

* * * *

Nothing's changed. Everything looks exactly like it used to then. Why did you fall in love with Andras? He didn't deserve you! The only thing that mattered to him was what was in it for him. Those rings… he made them especially for a chosen few. I pleaded with him to make one for me as well, but he refused, saying I had to prove myself first!

Aksel had vowed to never return to the old neighborhood, yet he yearned to see where Ingrid had lived before he executed the last installment of the plan. *You and that bastard turned my daughter against me! No matter how hard I tried to be who you and the others wanted me to be, all of you despised me, making me feel worthless and a loser with no future ahead of me.*

He'd spent years reliving what happened that night and planning his next move. It was time to move on but not until he got his final revenge. *Fleming and Xander never knew what was coming, but you always knew I'd not let you escape alive after I shot your lover! He was much too persuasive, making you do whatever he demanded! By the time he tricked me out of my share of that break-in money, you depended on drugs to survive from one day to the next, fully conscious of letting yourself and our daughter down because of your inability to break free from that man! I loved you yet you wouldn't let me be part of your and our child's lives. I begged you to give me another chance but you laughed at me. No one makes fun of me!*

He recalled the ugly scene when she'd seen her dead lover. *You screamed at me, saying I meant nothing to you. No one rejects me, not after what I went through! First with my father, then my brother and the syndicate. I'm pleased you're dead.*

Still as furious as he was then, he started the engine and drove off, hours later parking the car in a side street. As soon as he killed the remaining people, he'd get peace of mind. Bursting into tears, thinking about the daughter he'd never known, wondering if he was capable of killing his own flesh and blood, he suddenly laughed out loud. "It serves you right for not looking for me and for rejecting me just like the others."

Sitting in his car for what felt like an eternity, pushing feelings of remorse to the back of his mind, he turned the car around and headed back to Oslo and the last installment of the plan.

CHAPTER SEVENTEEN

"I THOUGHT I made it clear last time you called, I want nothing to do with you!" Joel's mother spat in his face and tried to close the door. Pushing her aside, Joel wiped the spit off his face with the back of his hand and entered the dark hall.

He'd expected her reaction and said, "I'm not here to visit. I just need answers to prevent more killings, and you'll provide them whether you like it or not!"

When he and Daniel left Bergen and moved to Oslo, they had brought nothing except clothes, a few possessions and their measly share from the dealings the syndicate paid them after they refused to deal in drugs and more break-ins. Taking a closer look at the woman in front of him, same tacky long black skirt, stained woolly jumper and dirty limp gray hair, he felt just as nauseous as he used to each time she came near him. He'd come a long way since then, eyes lingering on the broken mirror and dusty chest of drawers behind her.

"How dare you come here and threaten me? Why, you didn't even bother to give me money to pay my bills. What kind of son rejects his own mother?"

The wailing voice and puffy light brown eyes, made him nauseous. It didn't surprise him she wore the same old cardigan falling apart in the seams and dirty clogs he recalled from his childhood.

"I couldn't care less about what happens to you. All you have to do is answer my questions. If you do, I'll give you some money. It pleases me you'll be living here until you take your last breath. I hope memories of what you let that man to do to us, your own sons, haunt you in your grave!"

She giggled and reached for his jacket pocket. "Give me my money first, or I won't tell you anything."

He pushed her away from him. "You'll get nothing unless you give me what I came for. When we're through you'll never see me again."

"Get on with it, ask me what you want and give me my money!" she shouted, the same wicked smile he remembered from the past.

Wishing he was anywhere except there, he looked straight into her eyes. "When was the last time you heard from my brother?"

Taking a step closer to him, reeking of old booze, she flashed him another smile. "Why do you want to know? Your brother's been good to me. I wish he was here instead of you!"

"You don't give a damn about either of us! The only thing you care about is yourself and drinking yourself into oblivion. Where does he live? Don't lie to me; I know you visited him in the hospital."

"Sure, but that was ages ago. He was depressed, threatening to kill himself after that bitch broke up with him and got involved with another man. He begged me to let him stay the night a couple of times, then left. I'd not seen or heard from him until recently, when he called me unexpectedly. Nothing he told me made sense; he was in one of his usual weird moods, the kind that make him sound like a lunatic, which he is. I've nothing more to tell you; give me my money!"

"Not yet, I've got one more question for you. Think carefully before you respond. Did Aksel mention anything about wanting to settle an old score?" So much depended on her response, Joel's eyes bored into hers, heart pounding in his chest.

"He told me he was planning to finish killing the people who betrayed him. I don't suppose you know who they are."

Eyes locking with hers, he smiled and replied, "But I do, Mor. One of them is your granddaughter, the girl you never knew existed and whose life you'll never be part of. She's my niece and I'll do whatever it takes to protect and keep her alive. The cycle of abuse stopped with me and my brother. You'll not see or hear from me ever again."

He was halfway out of there when he heard her scream, "Give me my money. I kept my end of the bargain."

Turning to look at the pathetic creature, he pulled out some coins from his inner trouser pocket and threw them at her. "Take it, you'll not get another krona from me!"

Bending to pick up the coins from the floor, she screamed, "Goodbye and good riddance!"

He was sitting in his car when he heard her slam the front door shut and lock it. All he had to do now was find his sick brother before he tracked them down and got his wish. Leaving nothing to chance, Joel headed back to Oslo that night.

Chapter Eighteen

IT WASN'T UNTIL he returned home and was lying in his bed, trying to make sense of everything that Joel thought about his father's old cabin in the Nordmarka Forest, a short drive away. Situated in a beautiful part of the deep countryside, the spectacular scenery and landscape were the perfect antidote to a stressful city life. Recalling the times he and Axel spent there with the father who had made their lives a living hell, Joel made the decision to travel there in the morning. Winter had arrived and the weather forecast predicted heavy snowfall that week. He fell into a restless sleep, consumed by the fear that his brother was out there somewhere planning his next move, and slept until the sound of his mobile woke him up.

It was Daniel. "Where the hell are you? You can't expect me to wait for your call! Astrid's just received a letter with her morning post. Some anonymous lunatic's threatening her, saying she's not got long to live."

Shocked that everything he'd feared was happening so fast, Joel told him he was on top of things, then told his friend what he knew. "I visited my mother, she confirmed my suspicions. My brother's behind the killings, Daniel. Tell her I'll be with you soon. I'm on my way to Nordmarka and my father's old cabin. Please don't ask me to explain; everything will be revealed soon."

"Your brother's behind the killings? I can't believe the little boy we used to look out for when he was bullied on the playground is a killer. What's this got to do with him? I don't understand. And why are you driving to your father's cabin?" He couldn't get his head around the reason his friend had visited the woman who never gave a damn about him and his brother. They'd made a pact to never return home after arriving in Oslo.

"Trust me on this, Daniel. It was him all along; my sick, damaged brother killed them. I've yet to discover the reason and details. We're next, me, you and Astrid. I believe he's her father. Please don't tell her, not yet! She's my niece and I only figured it out a while back. All of it's starting to make sense. My brother had a fling with her mother until she ended it and became involved with Andras. He's sick, Daniel. I've got to find him before he kills again. Our father destroyed him."

"You seriously believe he killed those people? My God, what will you do now?" Daniel was trembling inside, thinking about the young boy no one understood or wanted to play with. The boy who shunned human contact and closeness. It must have destroyed him when the woman he loved turned her back on him.

"I left Ingrid when she needed me the most. If only I had known how unhappy and scared she must have been. I'd have brought her and her daughter with me to Oslo."

"I know how you feel. Maybe if I'd done the same with my brother, he'd have turned out differently. Are you okay?"

"Not really. I never looked back. If I had, I'd never have been capable of getting on with my life. It's too late for regrets. Be careful. You're dealing with a dangerous killer. Don't worry about me and Astrid, just watch your back."

"I promise. Just make sure you and she are safe. Don't let her out of your sight. You two are the only people I care about."

"I will. Keep me posted on everything." Ending the call, Daniel immediately dialed senior officer Morten Knudsen's number.

Answering on the first ring, Knudsen asked, "What can I do for you, Mr. Holst?"

"I've just talked with my security man. He knows who killed Fleming and Xander, officer. You must make sure

Astrid's safe. Joel thinks the killer is his brother. His name is Aksel Wranger, and Joel's pretty sure he's Astrid's father too. I've got nothing more to tell you. He's on his way to Nordmarka as we speak. He thinks his brother might be hiding in the forest in their father's old cabin. Please send officers there as fast as you can."

Knudsen opened the full report of the victims in the old Bergen case. It was very brief and sketchy. The investigation clearly had not been very thorough. Knudsen was not surprised by this. Murders of crime syndicate members were not a high priority in an overburdened police department. If there were any witnesses, they were too afraid to come forward, and the killers typically left few clues. So some investigators merely went through the motions, did the bare minimum, and moved the cases off their desks as soon as possible.

He browsed the file, then returned to a neighbor's statement. The female victim's name was Ingrid Jensen. Her next door neighbor had a daughter who attended the same class as Ingrid's daughter, Astrid. The neighbor said Ingrid had an affair with a man named Aksel who abused her and after breaking up with him she'd been involved with a younger man. Aksel kept visiting her against her wish, threatening to kill her unless she ended the new relationship. The neighbor had looked after the daughter each time her friend requested it.

Closing the computer, Knudsen tried to piece together the missing pieces of the old case. The girl never got to know her mother's ex, the man Joel Wranger claimed was the killer. He wondered if Wranger knew the reason he killed those people...

Reopening the file on his computer, he found the final piece of evidence linking it all together. No one had bothered to follow up on this information at the time. The birth certificate stated Astrid's father's name: Aksel Wranger. "We've at long last discovered the killer's identity. Holst was right calling me and owning up to what he knows."

Knudsen called the officer he had spoken to in Bergen, and updated him on recent events, instructing him to keep the news to himself. "We've got a dangerous psychopath on the loose! If the media hears about it there's no telling what might happen. I'm on my way to Nordmarka."

His conversation reminded him that he had an officer who had worked for the police in Bergen several years before. He was older, just about ready to retire, but he knew a lot about Bergen and Sandviken, and might be helpful on this case. He summoned the officer, briefed him on the case, and handed him the files.

The officer's reaction was strangely emotional, and he insisted on accompanying Knudsen to Nordmarka. Knudsen didn't have time to think about it further. They had to get there soon.

They dressed warmly for the trip and were halfway there when they decided to stop for a short break at a petrol station. The forecast was right, predicting more snow and freezing temperatures.

Returning to the car, they finished their black coffee and took another look at his notes. It didn't surprise Knudsen that Joel had wanted Daniel to keep his mouth shut. *Aksel Wranger, I'm coming after you before you kill your own daughter, brother and brother's friend. This time you'll pay for what you've done.*

CHAPTER NINETEEN

"HOW LONG HAVE you known my father's identity?" Astrid asked, voice trembling. After much persuasion, she had managed to get the officer in charge of her security that day to open up about what he knew. She had called Daniel on his mobile just as he was thinking of driving to Nordmarka to catch up with his friend.

Hearing her sounding so upset stopped him in his tracks. Attempting to calm her down, he offered to come round and keep her company. "I'm sorry you had to hear it from an officer. What exactly do you know?"

"That my father killed those people and probably Mor as well and that I'm next in line to die. I'm traveling to Sandviken to visit our old neighbors. Bodil Lyng and her daughter Aase Lyng Bentson looked after me when Mor needed it. They were like my second family. I didn't keep in touch with them after my mother died and I was moved to a foster home in another area in Bergen. It was the loneliest I'd ever been. I missed my home and friends."

Stunned at hearing her mention the surname Lyng, Daniel asked, "Are you sure that's Bodil's real surname?" His head was spinning.

"Of course! I'd hardly forget my friends' names. Lyng was Bodil's surname, but sometimes she used Bentson too. That was Aase's father's surname. They weren't married, but sometimes it was just simpler for Bodil to use his last name. Why are you asking?"

"I don't think it's a good idea for you to visit them right now; the police won't permit you to leave with a killer on the loose. Please don't risk it. The killer's a very dangerous man seeking revenge for something that happened a long time ago. Your father's very sick. He thinks you abandoned him since your mother didn't permit him to see you. I'll be with you shortly."

He was desperate to call Knudsen, but his brain told him to wait a while longer.

"No! I have every right to visit my friends. I need to talk with them. Bodil used to tell me my mother was very depressed each time my father visited us and that she wanted nothing to do with him after they broke up. Apparently, he threatened to hurt her if she got involved with another man. I wonder if that's the reason he killed Andras. He was always nice to me and gave me lovely pieces of costume jewelry for my birthday and Christmas. He and Mor were deeply in love and didn't deserve to die! They could have been happy together."

Hearing her say that, Daniel wanted to tell her she was mistaken. Andras Lyng was a selfish man, who like her crazy father fell in love with her mother, yet the only person he truly cared for was himself.

Daniel had wasted years attempting to make sense of what had happened, and getting over his relationship with Ingrid. Pieces of fake jewelry could never make up for what those men put her through. He'd struggled to come to terms with not taking her and Astrid with him to Oslo yet knew deep inside he and Ingrid wouldn't have lasted. She'd been too damaged and frail and addicted to cocaine and antidepressants. Besides, she never felt about him the way she did for her young lover. Astrid and Andras were all she cared about.

"Since you're determined to visit them, I'll drive you there. Joel and the police made it clear you're not permitted to go anywhere on your own. You must inform the officer responsible for your safety we're visiting old friends in Sandviken. I'll be with you in ten minutes."

He ended the call before she had the opportunity to say no. Wondering whether he ought to contact Knudsen and Joel and let them know where they were heading, he decided against it there and then. If what his friend suspected turned out to be true, that Aksel Wranger was hiding in his father's old cabin, the police would be informed and arrest him.

Daniel needed answers. If Andras Lyng was related to Astrid's friends, that explained the reason they had been looking after her. *This is even more surreal than anything I've heard before and I should know, given my circumstances and everything I've endured. I wonder if Ingrid knew her lover and best friends were family.*

Throwing a few items of clothing and toiletries into a suitcase, he changed into a pair of black jeans, a heavy sweater and boots. It was getting cold outside and he recalled the weather forecast predicting heavy falls of snow. Ingrid's old neighbors probably knew the answers he needed. If Andras was their relative, surely the initial Bergen murder investigation would have mentioned it? Suddenly, Daniel couldn't help wondering whether those people who carried the same surname harbored ill feelings towards Ingrid's daughter.

Nah, I'm letting my imagination cloud my judgment. No one's as evil as that. If they were after revenge, they got it when her mother was killed. Unless, of course, they want the daughter to pay as well for her involvement with Andras. Pushing his suspicions to the back of his mind, driving the short distance to her flat, he arrived exactly ten minutes later, heart sinking when he saw Astrid looking so upset, pale, and teary-eyed.

Assisting her into his car, he placed her suitcase next to his in the back seat. "Try to get some rest while we drive to Sandviken and don't worry so much. Everything will turn out alright in the end. Did you call your friends and tell them we're coming?" he asked in a tense voice.

"Not yet. I'll call them later from the car."

"I'd rather you didn't. I have a feeling we're not welcome."

Staring at him in disbelief, she whispered, "Why?"

"I'm not sure yet. My gut instinct tells me your friends know more than they told the police back then." As he drove towards the place he'd left years ago, determined to find out what her friends had been hiding from her and the police, something deep inside him urged him to discover the truth before the killer got his wish. He suspected someone stoked Aksel's desire for revenge for the wrong reasons. Until they'd talked with the neighbors, there wasn't much point in getting Joel and Knudsen involved.

CHAPTER TWENTY

BODIL LOOKED SHOCKED and hostile when she saw Daniel and Astrid on her doorstep. "What brings you here after all those years?" She was tall and slim, with a slightly pointed nose, dark blue eyes and long, thick gray hair in plaits down her shoulders.

Daniel replied, "Aren't you pleased to see your old friend's daughter?"

She hissed, "Why are you pestering me? There's nothing here for you anymore! Aase moved to Troldhaugen after she got a position at the Edvard Grieg Museum years ago. She was always enthralled by him, and who can blame her? He's Norway's most famous composer."

She took a closer look at the young girl she'd cared for a long time ago, and softened when she saw Astrid's tear-swollen face. "Would you like to get in touch with her? Aase misses your friendship."

Shaking her head, Astrid avoided Bodil's eyes.

"Why not? The two of you were very close, almost like sisters. I'm expecting visitors soon, so please tell me why you're here." She looked straight into Daniel's eyes.

"We've traveled all the way from Oslo to ask you some questions. Are you by chance related to Andras Lyng?"

He sensed how tense his question made her. She made a nervous attempt to smile, but he could see how scared she was.

"Lyng's hardly an unusual surname! You're seriously telling me you've come here to ask me something as dumb as that?" Eyes narrowing, she stepped aside to let them into the dark hall.

Following her, Daniel said, "Maybe, but it's a strange coincidence, wouldn't you agree? What was he to you? Unless you tell me the truth, I'll inform the police! You're obviously aware of the Oslo police officer who recently persuaded the Bergen police to reopen the old murder case in Sandviken. They've reason to believe the recent killings in Oslo are connected with it."

Face crumpling, Bodil replied nervously, "Come into the kitchen. I'll make us coffee. We'll talk properly there."

"That's not necessary, we're not here to socialize, please just answer my questions. If you lie to us, you'll regret it."

"You'd better get on with it before my visitors arrive. Just bear in mind I don't take orders from you and anyone else!"

"If you give us answers, we'll be out of here soon." Eyes boring into hers, he asked again, "Was he your relative?"

Her eyes welled up with tears, and her voice faltered. "Why do you want to know?"

"I'm asking the questions here, not you! Unless you tell me the truth, I'll call the police!" he shouted at her, feeling increasingly agitated.

"Andras was my brother. He and I lost touch for a very long time, long before he was killed. Ingrid was my neighbor and friend back then. If I had known what would happen to him, my own brother, I'd have warned him to stay away from her! I never got the chance to prevent his murder!"

"But the police must have questioned you and all the other neighbors," said Daniel. "How did they not figure out you were his sister? You had the same last name."

"The police!" she spat. "They didn't care. They didn't even try to solve the case. To them, Andras was just another casualty of the wars between crime syndicates. When they asked my name, I told them I was Bodil Bentson. They never checked and never made a connection."

"Do you still harbor bad feelings towards Ingrid?" Daniel asked. "Perhaps extending to being behind the killings, then and now? Andras was a low life, getting pleasure from robbing people and dealing drugs! Innocent people suffered because of him and the other members of the syndicates. I and my friend left the dealings behind and started fresh in Oslo. Fortunately for us, we never participated with heavy stuff, only a few break-ins. I'm not proud of what I've done but at least I never hurt anyone and I gave my share to Ingrid, who needed it more than I did."

"You're wrong about him! My brother was just a kid and respected jeweler designing costume jewelry. He didn't know what he was getting into when he got involved with her. She wormed her way into his heart and trousers! He was the biggest loser, not her!" Bodil started to cry.

Astrid asked, "How come you hate me and Mor so much? She never spoke badly about you and Aase."

"That's because she had no reason to badmouth either of us. Ingrid deserved what was coming to her! If Andras hadn't gotten involved with her, he'd still be alive now."

Astrid whispered, "You told me you cared for us. I don't understand why you didn't show your true feelings then."

Silencing her with his eyes, Daniel asked, "Were you behind Elias and Corey's killings? The murderer is a very sick person; you of all people know what kind of person we're dealing with. If it's the person we suspect, you're well aware of how vulnerable he is. In the state he's in, it's easy to put things into his head, making him do what you want."

Tears streaming down her face, Astrid cried, "I thought you cared about us! We trusted you. Mor must have known you were related to him. Everything I believed is a lie! Why did everyone hide the truth from me?"

Bodil reached for her hand but drew back when she saw the expression of hatred in Astrid's eyes. "You knew how scared Mor was of my father, yet you said nothing!" Astrid grabbed her by the throat, shouting, "How can you live with yourself knowing you did nothing to warn us! Mor would be alive now if you had informed her how much my father hated your brother. Answer me!"

Breaking free from Astrid's grip, Bodil screamed, "I'm glad she's dead! Why the hell did you have to come here? Andras was my brother, I let him down. After he was convicted for breaking into people's homes and smuggling fake jewelry and drugs, I cut him out of my life. Aase never forgave me; her uncle was the only father figure she had after her father died shortly after she was born. When she discovered how Andras died, she refused to have anything more to do with me and only calls once a year on my birthday. All of it is Ingrid's fault!"

Suddenly, before Daniel had the opportunity to stop her, Bodil said, "Aksel Wranger's your father! He killed your mother and my brother. Aksel couldn't bear losing her to Andras. Back then your father was a good-looking man, and he was infatuated with Ingrid. He somehow found out she had a baby and figured out you were his daughter. She was terrified he'd harm you and asked me to look after you when she suspected he was in the vicinity. Back then, Aksel was in and out of the mental hospital. After each treatment he'd visit her, hoping to get a glimpse of you. My brother was an idiot, yet in his own misguided way cared for both of you. One bullet in his head was all it took and he was gone. We never had the opportunity to reunite. Your mother knew how much Aksel hated Andras. I'll never forgive her for putting his life at risk!"

Astrid sobbed. "You pretended to care for us. What about me, what have I done to deserve your anger? Did you ever consider my feelings and wonder what happened to me? After I found out Mor died, I thought she'd killed herself... No one told me the truth... I was placed with foster parents. They were kind to me but they didn't love me like a biological child. My whole life's been a lie. I never had the opportunity to say goodbye to my mother."

Flashbacks of how desperate and lonely she'd felt at the time made her cry even harder. Growing up without her mother and having to fend for herself had nearly destroyed her. In her late teens she'd met and fallen in love with a boy who attended the same painting class. They dated for a short period of time. She put up with his advances, even though she was inwardly repulsed by intimacy with him, vividly recalling all the men who came and went in her mother's life. Every man her mother became involved with sooner or later betrayed and left her. Astrid vowed not to let a man inside her heart and life, her only focus to revenge Daniel for leaving her mother. Life was easier and less complicated when she shut out other people and especially men from her life.

"You look just like her," Bodil hissed. "Same blue eyes, same curly blonde hair, same figure. I hated you! All of it was a pretense. Aase was the only one who cared. Unlike me, my daughter's kind and loving."

Putting his face in his hands, Daniel asked, "She doesn't know the truth about what went on?" He was shocked to discover she was even more cruel than he'd suspected.

"Of course, not. As far as Aase's concerned, Ingrid and her uncle were unfortunate victims of brutal killings by members of criminal gangs. I didn't tell her about it until she was old enough to comprehend. By then, Astrid lived in another part of Bergen."

Incensed by her callous attitude, Daniel replied in a stern voice, "She'll soon find out. Just tell me this: Do you suppose Aksel killed Ingrid because she'd witnessed your brother's murder?"

She looked straight into his eyes, replying, "Aksel's a lunatic. I have nothing to do with what goes on in his head."

"Fair enough, but it was you who initiated the other killings of Elias and Cory. Aksel wasn't capable of arranging it by himself. He's too damaged to plan something so devious. Did your resentment and anger over what happened to your brother eat you up inside? Is it also the reason you're making him come after his own daughter, me, and Joel because you want everyone associated with your brother's murder to suffer the same fate?"

Watching her eyes flare up, angry thin mouth and clenched hands, he wasn't in the least shocked by her response. "He and only he made the decision to kill those people. He'll never admit to anything else. I have no idea what he's planning next."

She was cold, calculating, and completely devoid of compassion and empathy. If what he suspected was true, that Bodil had persuaded Aksel to kill those men, she wouldn't hesitate to talk him into killing the three people he held responsible for rejecting and destroying him. Aksel was merely a slave, obeying her instructions, a puppet dancing to her tune. Just thinking about it made him nauseous. He wanted to wring her neck for deciding who deserved to die. But without proof she was behind the killings and next stage of the plan, there wasn't much point involving the police yet.

"Think what you like! My poor brother would be alive now if it wasn't for your bitch of a mother!" Taking a step closer to the woman she'd known since she was born, Bodil slapped her face, screaming, "I wish you and that bitch of a mother of yours were never born!"

Punching her stomach, Daniel watched her fall down on the floor, shouting at her, "You're behind the recent killings! I'll make sure you pay for it." Taking Astrid's hand in his, he held her close, saying "We're through here. I'm here for you and won't let anything bad happen to you."

Slamming the front door behind them, Daniel knew he'd never forgive himself if something happened to Astrid. It was too late to save Ingrid, but he had to make sure her daughter was safe; he owed Ingrid that much.

CHAPTER TWENTY-ONE

DESPERATE TO FIND out if his brother was hiding inside the cabin or at least to find clues to where he might be, Joel called Knudsen and asked him to meet him there as soon as he arrived in Nordmarka. After he gave him the address, Knudsen said, "I'll alert my colleagues to send out officers to search your father's cabin. I'm bringing another officer with me who used to live in Bergen and work for the police there. He might be able to shed some light on the case. If your brother's inside the cabin, you must let me know immediately. The weather's preventing us from getting there for at least another hour."

Joel found the spare key to the front door under the mat. Something didn't sit right with him. Aksel had been infatuated with Ingrid, repeatedly asking her out, and when she accepted his invitation to dinner he'd been ecstatic. Astrid was his daughter, so why would he want to kill her?

Entering the large room, comprising a kitchen sink, small bathroom behind the large wooden table, and armchair, he was instantly transported to another time, when he and his brother spent time there with the alcoholic father who abused them and constantly argued with their mother and his equally drunk friends.

Feeling a mixture of sadness and anger, Joel caught a glimpse of himself in the cracked mirror on the wall in the far corner, haggard face and puffy eyes proof of how much he'd been worrying about revisiting the place where his father spent months on end without telling them where he was.

Eyes falling on the black sack beside him on the floor, he opened it and rummaged through the old papers and magazines that must have been left there for a very long time. Emptying the contents, he watched it scatter. He noticed something stuck between two floor boards. *I'll be damned if it isn't Far's old wristwatch, the one his parents gave him when he turned eighteen, what the hell is it doing there? He never went anywhere without it.*

Venturing outside into the deep snow, he found a branch that had fallen off a tree by the gate, picked it up, and returned inside. Sitting on the floor, he twisted it to fit between the boards and managed to slide it further down, hooking the watch and lifting it up. Looking at it, he saw the familiar name engraved on the inside of the strap, Stein Wranger. Perhaps it fell off his wrist when he was fighting with one of his friends. He might have been too drunk to care. *But if he did, surely, he'd have done the same as I did now, unless…*

He felt sick, just thinking about it. Was it possible Aksel had prevented him and killed him? If that was true, where had he disposed of the body? Running into the bathroom, retching over the sink, he was relieved he'd hardly eaten that day, Joel cried.

Their father had left them years ago, and they had never discovered what happened to him. Aksel had vanished around the same time. What if Aksel had found him here and killed him? Mor never gave a damn about him. Relieved he was gone and out of her life, she didn't bother to report him missing to the police.

Joel returned to the floor and started to lift off one board at the time, then jumped down onto the damp ground, relieved he was wearing thick gloves and boots and had brought a torchlight so he could see clearly in the dark. His eyes fell on a pile of garbage in the right corner. Poking at the contents with the stick he'd used earlier until it fell apart and scattered on the ground he started to sob uncontrollably when he saw the dismembered body parts that must have been lying there for ages, thinking, *Oh, Aksel, what have you done?* All of it made sense now: his father's missing watch and not knowing what became of him when he didn't return home.

Hours later, sitting at the old table, with Knudsen and the older officer he had brought with him, Joel knew without a doubt his brother had killed their father.

Looking just as shocked, Knudsen said, "It's fortunate I arrived sooner than I thought. Officers are outside searching the grounds." Yawning after the long drive, he gestured at the black bin bags by the door. "If what you suspect is true, your brother's a very dangerous man. From what you've just told me about him and what he did to the two of you, I'm not surprised he had it coming. Still, shooting him in the head and sawing off his body parts, I never saw anything as brutal as that during my time on the force."

Too distraught to respond, Joel shook his head in despair. "Aksel was Far's favorite punching bag. Me? I just accepted what was in store for me. At least I had Daniel to turn to for support; my brother's younger than me and had no one. Everyone used to laugh at him at school, calling him a weirdo and bullying him every chance they got. I let him down... my own brother. Leaving him behind to fend for himself without someone to care for him and make sure he got the help he needed. All I could think of at the time was getting away from the inferno that was my existence. Daniel and I vowed to never look back."

Feeling even more nauseous than when he'd discovered his father's remains, Joel ran out of there into the deep snow outside, attempting to make sense of what had happened. Breathing in the fresh cold air, he saw Knudsen and the older officer follow him outside. He told them, "Daniel messaged me. He and Astrid visited her old neighbor in Sandviken. He suspects she's behind the Oslo killings. They're on their way here."

"Astrid's coming here?" the other officer asked. Something in the way his voice cracked made Joel turn to face the man. He was bald and had sharp blue eyes that held a look of shock and deep emotion. Joel asked him, "What's your name? I don't recall you giving it to me."

Tears welling up in his eyes, the officer replied in a sad voice, "My name's Arvid, Arvid Jensen."

Stunned by his response, Joel whispered, "But that's the same surname as Astrid and Ingrid. It's a common Norwegian name but no coincidence, right? Surely, you're not related?"

Looking straight into his eyes, Arvid replied in a voice hoarse with emotion, "I wasn't sure at first when Knudsen told me about the case. But when I saw the file, I knew it was her … my little girl… murdered in her own home in Sandviken. The file had a photo of her and that creep, and I knew it had to be her. I had an affair with her mother many years ago before I moved to Oslo, away from all the gossips. Bergen's a small place, word goes around and before we had the opportunity to sort out our future, Bjørg made the decision to stay with her husband. She never told me she was pregnant with our child. It took years to get over her. She was the love of my life and still is.

"When an officer I used to work with in Bergen joined the force in Oslo where I was working, he told me about my daughter, the baby Bjørg gave birth to. Her husband was infertile so he knew the child wasn't his, so he insisted she be sent away. Back then, it was unthinkable for a married woman to leave her husband and get pregnant by another man, no matter how unhappy she was with him. She contacted social services who placed the child in care and found foster parents. I found the record of her birth, and saw that Bjørg had put my name on the birth certificate as the father. I never knew about my daughter's whereabouts until she was eight years old, when I found out where she was. I was living in Oslo and made the decision to not interfere in her life but I kept an eye on her until she turned eighteen. After that, I just lost track of her. It's my biggest regret I never got to know my own flesh and blood. Finding out she was killed nearly destroyed me. Not a day goes by when I don't think about what might have been."

Speechless, Joel went inside, sat down by the table, and buried his face in his hands. The officer working on both murder cases was Ingrid's father and Astrid's grandfather. Suddenly, a scary thought entered his mind. Jumping off his chair, he heard Arvid say, "I know what you think. Your brother doesn't know about me. I want it to stay that way for now. It's also the reason I didn't give you my name at first."

"What happens now? What if Daniel's right about Ingrid and Astrid's old neighbor? If she made him kill those men, how will we be able to stop him coming after Astrid, me and Daniel? He's a very sick man. I've known it for a long time."

Arvid said in an angry voice, "You ought to have taken my daughter and granddaughter with you to Oslo! At least you and your friend knew the man Ingrid was involved with. I never got the chance to protect her!"

Crying openly, Joel sobbed, "You're right. We were immature and selfish leaving them behind. Both of us spent years regretting it, wishing we could go back and put things right. Hindsight is a wonderful thing, officer... Arvid... What truly matters now is to make sure Astrid's safe and make my brother confess about Bodil's part in the killings and obtain evidence to convict her. Have you any idea how to get him to confess what they've done?"

"We've got to make him believe his daughter wants to meet him," said Knudsen. "She'll be the bait that forces him to come out from where he's hiding. It's a lot to ask after everything she's been through but it's our best hope."

Joel nodded. "You're right. Daniel and I made a terrible mistake not bringing them with us to Oslo. I pray Astrid's life will not be at risk." Suddenly, his own life meant very little compared with hers. He felt certain his friend felt the same way.

CHAPTER TWENTY-TWO

AASE LYNG BENTSON was stunned to find out Astrid and Daniel had visited her mother after all those years. "How come you're so keen I contact her, Mor? It's been so long since we saw each other." After her friend's mother died, the two girls hardly saw each other and when Astrid was placed in a foster home, they'd lost touch. Plagued with memories of her late uncle and their closest friends, she never understood her mother's unwillingness to talk about the young girl whose life had changed because of what happened one fatal night. Sitting on the living room couch, where she'd spent hours on end playing with her friend after school, Aase felt the same migraine coming on whenever she saw and spent time with her mother.

"You must call immediately and tell her that her father wants to meet her," Bodil replied.

"Why now all of a sudden? I can't force her to meet the man that killed her mother! Besides, it's nothing to do with me, Mor. What's the real reason you want them to meet? I was under the impression you wanted me to visit because you've missed me. Aksel killed your brother! Have you forgotten how devastated you were when you found out about it?"

She loathed the feeble-minded man who had killed her uncle. Andras was the closest thing to a father she'd ever had since her father wasn't alive. After he and Ingrid became an item, Aase spent more time at her friend's house than her own home. Over the years, Aase distanced herself from her mother, relieved they lived far apart from each other.

Bodil had never recovered from what happened to her brother, and Aase believed her mother suffered with severe depression yet refused to admit she needed help. Lately, Bodil called her daughter nearly every day, saying she was lonely and had nothing to live for. Worst of all, she blamed Ingrid for her brother's murder. Suddenly, despite having cut him out of their lives when she found out about his criminal activities, she'd been adamant her old friend was responsible for what happened to him.

Repeating her question, Aase said. "Well, what's your answer? Why are you so determined that Astrid be reunited with her father? He's and dangerous man, and she hasn't seen him since she was very young. If I were her, I'd never want anything to do with the man who killed my mother."

Smiling at her, Bodil said, "You're so beautiful, Aase, with your long blonde hair. You have my blue eyes. I've got something to tell you. Please hear me out. It's the main reason I wanted to see you, apart from missing and loving you."

Expecting Bodil to say she was ill, Aase asked in a scared voice, "What is it? You've changed and seem more depressed since we last met. We used to tell each other everything when I was a child. Why are you so determined I get in touch with Astrid?"

Kissing her cheek, Bodil cried, "Everything's Ingrid's fault! Aksel loathed every man she was involved with. Andras didn't stand a chance. She rejected the father of her child! Astrid's just the same, not wanting anything to do with her father. Aksel's ill; after what his father did to him and his brother it's hardly surprising he's not right in the head. When we bumped into each other in Sandviken last year, he told me he'd recently been discharged from the psychiatric department and wanted to meet his daughter. He said a friend told him she'd moved to Oslo. Her foster parents used to be his friends, and they told him they'd never adopted her because she refused to accept them as her parents. She told them that even though they'd been good to her, they could never replace her mother.

"Aksel must get the chance to meet her and get to know her. After killing Andras, he's indebted to us! He must kill her and those two men. Daniel and Joel left and started fresh in

Oslo, leaving me behind to relive what happened that night! Neither of them deserves to live! I loathe her just as much as her mother."

Shaking, she cried, "You can't imagine what it was like to see my own brother murdered. Please say you'll call her."

Frightened and angry, Aase raised herself from the couch, shaking her head. "No! I'll not call her because you want him to kill her. Astrid's my friend. What happened then wasn't her fault! She was just a kid who lost her mother. You've no right dictating who lives and dies. Andras' murder was tragic but that's no reason to kill innocent people. Answer me truthfully. Did you persuade Aksel to kill those men in Oslo? Are you behind his plan to kill his own daughter and her friends?"

Aase had made a new life for herself in Troldhaugen, working as curator in the Edvard Grieg Museum. Suddenly, everything made sense. Her mother had wanted her to move away from Sandviken so she wouldn't be there when she and that vile man conspired to murder those people. They both blamed those men and Astrid for their miserable existence and wanted revenge.

"God help you, Mor, for what you've done! We must call the police and inform them of everything you've planned with that man. Can't you see you've been punishing the wrong people? Aksel killed Andras! Astrid and those men are innocent."

Bodil screamed, "I've hated them too long to stop now." Getting up from the couch, reaching for Aase's hand, she cried, "Please don't leave me… You're all I have."

Pushing her away, Aase shouted, "You're dead to me after what you've done! I knew you were sick, but I never imagined you were capable of murder!"

Close to fainting, Bodil fell in a heap on the floor, crying, "Andras was the only person I counted on to look after us. When he died I had no one to comfort and support me. That bitch was his biggest mistake! I'll never be able to move on and heal unless Aksel kills her daughter and those men. All of them are guilty of betraying my brother and robbing us of him."

Looking down at her mother, Aase hissed, "Those men were members of the same gangs Andras was involved with! They didn't make Aksel kill him. Astrid's an innocent victim in all of this, just like we are!"

Shocked and scared for her friend, she paced the room, then returned to her mother, saying, "Aksel's a psychopath; what's your excuse? You've tricked him into committing those crimes and you're still doing it! I know everything there is to know about your precious brother! He was good to us but he was also a hardened criminal who exploited people to get what he wanted: enough money to last him a lifetime and women who were too weak to stand up to him. You did the right thing, cutting him out of our lives! When he was killed your grief clouded your judgment. Suddenly, the criminal that was your brother and my uncle turned into an innocent victim and a saint.

"Can't you see? Andras cared for us and Ingrid when it suited him! The only person he truly cared about was himself. He and Ingrid would never have lasted. Sooner or later he'd have left her and us, and gotten himself involved with another woman and more crime. After everything you've done, I want nothing more to do with you. I wish you were dead. At least then I would be able to move on without the shame of having a murderer for a mother! Aksel murdered your brother, yet you're obsessed with revenging innocent people through him... Aksel may have pulled the trigger but you are just as guilty as him for making him do it!"

It was too late to get through to her. Bodil was beyond help and just as disturbed as her accomplice.

Getting up from the floor, Bodil staggered into the kitchen and pulled out a pair of scissors from the bottom drawer by the sink. With her right hand she stabbed them into her chest, blood oozing from the deep wound through her white blouse, down her long black skirt, bare legs and feet, her mouth turning blue.

Desperate to save her from dying, Aase grabbed a kitchen towel from the top shelf and pressed it against the wound, crying "Please don't die on me, Mor. If only I'd known how badly Andras' death affected you. You ought to have confided it to me instead of resorting to such desperate measures!"

Watching her mother fall down on the floor, Aase sat next to her, one hand pressing against the towel on her chest, the other reaching for her bag on the chair at the table, pulling out her mobile and calling the Bergen Police, requesting they come and send an ambulance. "My mother's badly injured! She stabbed herself in the chest with a pair of scissors! This is our address, please come as quickly as you can before she dies!"

Later that day, after her mother's life was saved by doctors and nurses in the emergency room in the local hospital, Aase was relieved to hear her confess her part in the killings. Walking up to her bed, she said, "I'm pleased you're alive and owned up to what you've done. Goodbye, Mor, I never want to see you again."

Leaving before her mother had the opportunity to respond, Aase thanked the officer for offering to drive her to the station where she'd catch a train back to Troldhaugen. She prayed her childhood friend would be safe and looked forward to calling her in the near future.

Chapter Twenty-Three

"I'M YOUR GRANDDAUGHTER? But you're a police officer, and Mor never mentioned you!" Shocked, she had never known of him until now, Astrid felt even more bereft. Not only had she lost her mother but this man claiming to be her grandfather had never bothered to get in touch with them. "Mor never mentioned you, she must have known who her father was. Are you sure we're related?"

She was close to having a mental breakdown. Too much had happened lately, discovering her father's identity and his wish to kill her and now this complete stranger informing her he was her grandfather. Looking at him, she attempted to find any similarities between them, facial features and mannerisms yet she couldn't except for his eyes. He had the same shade of blue eyes as Astrid and her mother.

They were in his office at the station, sitting opposite each other at his desk. Taking a deep breath, Arvid sighed and said,

"Yes, I'm certain we're family. Please hear me out. Your grandmother, her name's Bjørg, was the love of my life and always will be. Sadly, she passed away years ago, but I know how happy she'd have been to know you. Ingrid's the product of our love for each other. We had an affair, which I'm not proud of, but Bjørg was separated from her husband when we met and later returned to him.

"Back then, women were expected to stay in a bad relationship and she felt guilty for betraying him. I didn't find out she was pregnant with our child until much later from an old colleague who knew her and her husband. Her husband knew Ingrid wasn't his and made Bjørg send the child away. I searched for her when I found out about her. By the time I found her, she was living in a loving foster home and she was already eight years old. Her foster parents didn't want to tell her about me or let me visit her. They were good people, and I didn't want to interfere with her life, so I stayed away and just kept track of her from afar."

Sad to hear her mother had never met her biological father, and that they'd lived in fear of Astrid's father with no one to protect and care for them, Astrid covered her ears with her hands. "This is too awful to be true! I don't want to talk to you anymore!"

Arvid said in a kind voice, "I know it's a lot to take in and come to terms with. You must give yourself time to heal. Too much has happened in a relatively short space of time. My life changed when I discovered I had a daughter. My life has changed so much since then, but not a day passes when I don't think about the little girl I left behind in Bergen."

He went to her and put his arms around her. "I can't... won't... lose you as well!"

Overwhelmed by his spontaneous gesture, she felt safe for the first time since her mother died. So much had happened after she relocated to Oslo and started to work for Daniel. She'd been convinced he was the reason her mother's life had spiraled out of control after he'd abandoned her. She even blamed him for her mother's death and her own unhappiness.

Swallowing to rid herself of the big lump in her throat, eyes brimming with tears, she whispered, "If you had known where we were living, you might have been able to save her... Mor's gone; I'll never see her again. Neither of us will. I trusted Bodil, thinking she cared about us! Instead, she lied to me, saying she'd always look after me. I called Aase last night. One of the officers gave me her mobile number, saying you wouldn't mind since we go back a long time. She told me everything and that her mother attempted to kill herself. I hope she rots in hell for what she's done! I wish I knew then what I know now. Aase wants nothing more to do with her. At least she never lied to me."

Feeling his arms around her and knowing that he cared about her meant everything to her. She wasn't alone anymore. Her grandfather was there to protect and care for her. Weeping for what might have been if her mother was still alive, she withdrew from his embrace. "I was wrong about Daniel. He escaped from his past too. He and Joel left all the pain behind and started new lives in Oslo. Holst Enterprises is a testimony to human strength and new beginnings."

Smiling at her, Arvid filled in the gaps about recent events. "Daniel and Joel are worried sick about you. They both know they failed you and your mother, but they were desperate to leave behind the place that held so many bad, painful memories, and they were too immature to understand how dangerous your father was. Daniel cares deeply about you, and Joel's over the moon you're his niece.

"Elias Fleming and Cory Xander were members of several syndicates that smuggled fake jewelry and drugs in Norway and Scandinavia. Andras gave them identical rings he'd designed himself. They were tokens of his gratitude for delivering on services. Ingrid was just an innocent victim. She was desperately in love with a criminal whose sister had cut all ties with him when she found out about his crimes. After he died, his sister decided to avenge him to make up for her own feelings of guilt that she hadn't been there for him when he needed her.

"Andras wouldn't have given a damn about her if it had been the other way around. Cory didn't care about anyone apart from himself. Daniel's successes incensed him, hence the plan to destroy him by getting you to do his dirty work. He'd have talked you into destroying his company and both his and Joel's lives. We'll never know exactly what he had planned. He was insanely jealous of Joel for getting a high position as head of security. Cory and Elias were always resentful of Daniel and Joel and their new lives in Oslo.

"According to witnesses the Bergen police talked to when the old case was reopened, both men deliberately relocated to the capital to be close to the men they viewed as their enemies. Men who'd found success and managed to leave their past behind while Cory and Elias had to take occasional jobs for crime syndicates to scrape by...

"Envy is a terrible thing. It leads to all kinds of misery and destruction. When I realized the female victim in Bergen was my daughter, I was overcome with grief for the child I never got to know. When I realized she had a daughter, that I had a granddaughter, I was desperate to meet you and try to help you. You must put your trust in me and believe me when I say I'll always be here for you. I'd never willingly risk your life if I wasn't convinced what I'm about to ask of you is our best chance to capture your father and prevent more killings. I would gladly give up my life for you if the circumstances were different."

Anticipating his request, Astrid held his hand firmly in hers. "You propose I'm the bait that'll get my father to come out from where he's hiding."

He nodded. "I didn't like it when Knudsen came up with it, but I believe now it's our only chance."

"But how? No one knows where he is! What makes you think he wants to meet me?" Everything felt surreal, almost as if she were in a horror film where people chased her over something she wasn't guilty of.

"No matter how much he blames you for ostracizing him from your life, just like your mother, you're his daughter and he wants to know you. If we can make him believe you didn't know he existed until recently, and that you genuinely want to meet him, he might come forward."

"But that's insane! I already met him years ago in Sandviken! I just didn't know he was my father. I even suspected Daniel might be my father. It's the reason I didn't want to have a relationship with him but was determined to find out about his connection with my mother's death." She felt cheap just thinking about it. "I assume you've told him and Joel you're my grandfather?"

"Of course, I gave them a hard time, thinking especially Daniel could have saved Ingrid if he'd stuck around longer. But that was just wishful thinking. She fell in love with the wrong man, and put her trust in those awful people, your neighbor and members of the syndicates. I let my own daughter down. I won't make the same mistake with you! This is our plan:

"Joel told us your father is obsessed with technology, and most likely owns a computer and mobile. We want you to speak directly to him on the national TV news tonight. He's bound to be bored on his own and eager to watch the latest news and updates on the murder cases. Also, he must wonder what's happened to his accomplice. Bodil most likely kept in touch with him regularly to control his every move, especially their final installment of the plan.

"Will you be able to do what we ask? We've contacted his psychiatrist and asked him to suggest what to say. He agreed to put together words and phrases that'll convince him you genuinely want to meet him. There aren't any guarantees he'll believe you, but all you have to do is sound and look as if you mean it. If, and it's a big if, he feels convinced you're willing to let him into your life, he might cancel the final stage of the plan.

Trembling at the idea of what he expected from her, Astrid whispered, "I'll do what you ask of me... I'll be as convincing as you want me to be. What will happen to Bodil? I feel so sorry for her daughter. Just like me, Aase's just an innocent victim."

Arvid replied in a hard voice, "Bodil will be charged with planning the Oslo murders and persuading a dangerous psychopath to kill his own daughter and two men. She'll be sent to prison for a very long time. Given the fact that Aksel's a very sick man and has a track record of mental illness, he'll most likely be confined to a psychiatric unit for the rest of his life. I'm so very grateful you've consented to appear on the national news tonight. I'll inform my team to prepare everything."

Squeezing her hand, he said, "I'll be there watching over you and Knudsen will arrange around the clock protection for you and your friends. I give you my word I'll not let you down."

"I know you won't. Maybe, when all of it is over, we'll be able to continue getting to know each other? Mor never had the chance to meet and know you. She'd have been so happy knowing you care about and look after me. I very much want us to be part of each other's lives."

Tightening his gentle grip on her hand, Arvid looked her in the eyes. "No one and nothing will come between us ever again. I'll always be here for you when you need me. You're not on your own anymore."

"What will happen if he can't be persuaded to meet me? What will you do then?" Her mouth quivered.

"That's not an option. Aksel will come out of hiding and when all of this is behind us, we'll get on with our lives."

Yet no matter how hard he tried to convince her everything would turn out alright, he knew something could go wrong. And if something happened to her he'd not be able to continue. Pushing any doubts to the back of his mind, he started to focus on tonight's event.

CHAPTER TWENTY-FOUR

AKSEL COULD HARDLY believe it. Astrid Jensen was speaking directly to him on the evening news. Seeing her like that and so close up on the computer screen made him want to touch and be there with her. He'd been expecting Bodil's call to his mobile and final instructions on the last stage of the plan. When he didn't hear from her as arranged, he'd decided to watch the evening news on his computer, in case something had happened to her. Maybe she'd had an accident and was injured or worse, dead.

He recalled how angry she made him last time they spoke, warning him if he didn't obey her, she'd inform the police where he was hiding.

His eyes were glued to the screen and the young girl with the same color of hair and frightened eyes as her mother when she realized he was about to shoot her just like he had her lover. Aksel swore out loud. "She gave me no choice. I had to kill her after she saw me kill him! I'm so sorry, Ingrid, but you kept my daughter from me, refusing to let me see her and be part of her life."

Ever since he'd been living on his own, in and out of hospital and fending for himself, Bodil had talked him into doing things he wasn't convinced were right. Turning up the volume, he heard the girl say, "Please call me, I want to meet and talk to you. I never knew who you were when I was very young. When I found out about you, I knew I had to get in touch. My mobile number's on the screen. I want us to get to know each other. You're all I've got left after Mor died. I'm your daughter and unless you call me I'll spend the rest of my life wondering what might have been. I love you, Far. If you care about me, you'll get in touch tonight. Please don't let me down."

Writing her number on a note card, Aksel cried, "Bodil's wrong saying my own flesh and blood wants nothing to do with me! Astrid loves and needs me!" But a chilling thought suddenly occurred to him. *What if the police put her up to saying those things? Making her pretend she cares about me, and wants to meet me? I'm not a fool; she's not come forward until now.*

He howled at the screen, sitting by the window in his father's friend's cabin in Nordmarka, well aware the police had discovered his father's remains in the old cabin and were searching for him. "My little girl needs me! Why else would she talk to me on the news? Did the police talk her into helping them catch me? If I don't call her, she'll think I don't care!"

Staring at her face, same features and eyes as her mother, he switched off the computer, and paced the room. This could be his only chance to meet her. Surely, she wouldn't lie to her own father, pretending she cared when all she wanted was to help the police catch the man who killed her mother? Turning on the computer, Googling the latest news updates, he discovered his accomplice had been taken to the emergency room after she'd injured herself in her home earlier that week. His heart skipped a beat when he saw her name. The news bulletin said she was in stable condition and that further updates would be posted throughout the week.

Slamming his hand on the screen, Aksel screamed, "I hope you'll die just like the men you persuaded me to kill! Because of you I'm scared of meeting my daughter. I wish I'd never met you. That brother of yours was killed because of what he and Ingrid did behind my back! If it wasn't for you forcing me to kill again, the old case wouldn't have been reopened. Your constant interference in my life's causing me to hide from my own child! I'll not lose her because of you."

Everyone he'd ever known treated him like dirt and made fun of him, ridiculing and diminishing him every chance they had. First his father, who abused and forced him to do awful things, then his brother. Joel didn't keep in touch after he and

Daniel moved to Oslo. Aksel had called and visited his mother a few times over the years, but he realized the only thing that mattered to her was the money he gave her. "I ought to have killed her after I shot my father!" But she was too smart to come near Aksel, and fully aware of how volatile he was.

He'd outsmarted the old perverted bastard, making him believe he wanted to spend father and son time in the cabin, reminiscing about the past. Riddled with arthritis, he'd been too drunk to see through Aksel and what he had in store for the old man. It was child's play tricking him into the cellar, despite having to lift up the floor boards to get to it. *All I had to do was tempt him with more alcohol and he was putty in my hands. He never knew what was coming when I shot him in the head from behind.* Grimacing at the memory of all the blood, and dismembering his body with a saw, then hiding the remains under a pile of garbage, and returning upstairs to put back the floor boards, he suddenly remembered his father's old wristwatch. *It must have fallen off his wrist when I carried him... If the police found it they're welcome to it! It serves him right to be dead after what he did to me and my brother.*

Sitting in a corner in his friend's cabin, watching a rat brush past him, Aksel wiped the sweat off his face with his sleeve. *I'll risk it. I've got nothing to lose except my freedom. Bodil won't say anything against me after what she's done! My daughter needs me. I'll call her now on my mobile and ask her to meet me here. I'll load my gun in case the police follow her.* He had enough bullets to kill her friends and her if she tricked him.

Bodil's wrong about her, saying she hates and wants nothing to do with me. But she's right about those men. Joel and Daniel don't deserve to live after leaving me behind to survive on occasional jobs for the syndicates! My daughter loves me and can't wait to meet me! I'll never let you disappear from my life again.

Looking around him at the filthy floor and surfaces, and tacky pieces of furniture, he went into the equally dirty bathroom, determined to look his best for her.

"How do you feel, after speaking to him on national TV?" Arvid asked afterwards.

"What do you want me to say? I've just tricked my father into believing I care for him and want to meet him." Beside herself with worrying, she wondered if he'd call her that evening. If he did, she had no option but to play her part and meet him.

Arvid put an arm around her shoulder. "I'm so sorry you're in this awful situation. It's our only chance to catch him before he kills again."

"I know, but it doesn't make what I'm about to do easier. What will you do if he's seen through me and knows I've lied to him? He might set a trap for all of us. Where will you be when I meet him?" She was shaking like a leaf, teeth chattering inside her mouth.

Touching her face gently, he replied in a hoarse voice, "I'll be watching his every move and so will Daniel and Joel. Joel's certain he's hiding in their father's friend's cabin about an hour's drive from here in the Nordmarka Forest. If he's right we've got to drive there as soon as he calls you and invites you to meet him there. Just sit tight until he calls. All you have to do is to keep up the pretense and convince him that you love him. If he sees you're no threat to him and don't reject him like everyone else in his life, he won't have any reason to harm you."

Surprised Daniel and her newfound uncle wanted to be there for her, she asked, "How come they're willing to risk their lives for me?"

"Because they care about you and want you to be safe, and to know they're here for you. Daniel's very protective of you and Joel's family, just like me."

"Thank you. Maybe Mor didn't die in vain! And maybe nailing the man who killed her won't be as hard as I thought." Determined to go through with the ordeal, she asked, "Where are they now?"

Smiling, Arvid replied, "They're on their way to Nordmarka as we speak. Did I mention Bodil Lyng's been charged with being accomplice to murder? She was arrested in her home this morning."

"No, but I'm pleased she's not dead! It would have been too good for her after what she's done! You must promise me you'll make both of them pay for what they've done!"

Looking her in the eyes, Arvid said, "I give you my word even if it's the last thing I do before retiring from the force."

She was about to say something when her mobile rang in her bag. Pulling it out she answered after the third signal. Holding her breath, she heard him say, "Do you really mean what you said earlier today? I've waited so long to hear from you!"

Composing herself, she replied in a calm voice "Of course, we're family. A daughter needs her father. You've always been on my mind and in my heart. Please tell me when and where we can meet. We've wasted too long not having each other in our lives, Far."

She heard him sob at the other end of the line. He said in a voice thick with emotion, "This is the address. Please come here as soon as you can."

"I'll be with you very soon. Please be assured I'll drive there on my own, Far." She'd been reading her lines from the psychiatrist's notes.

"Good. I'll be here waiting for you, sweetie. Deep down, I always knew you were your daddy's girl."

Half an hour later, she was seated next to her grandfather, driving to Nordmarka. He said, "Daniel and Joel just arrived and have positioned themselves behind the cabin in the deep snow where he can't see them. Knudsen and his officers are also on their way. They should be there a little while before we arrive. They'll be watching over you from where they're hiding around the cabin. I'll drive you as close as I can without him noticing. After he lets you inside, you must tell him you've parked your car deep inside the forest where it can't be seen. We'll give you ten minutes maximum with him before joining you. Daniel's assured me he'd gladly die to make sure you're safe. Joel and I would as well."

Sitting with her own thoughts, praying all of them would be safe, she suddenly realized how much she cared for Daniel. She wondered if he felt the same deep connection between them yet wasn't sure what it meant yet.

CHAPTER TWENTY-FIVE

SHE'LL BE HERE SOON. I've got to clean this place until it shines. He found bottles of detergent and air freshener in the cupboard beneath the kitchen sink. Busying himself frantically cleaning the surfaces and scrubbing the floorboards with an old towel, he could hardly wait to see her. His little girl was arriving any minute. He'd at long last be part of her life. From now on, both their lives would change for the better. He'd never be alone and ridiculed anymore.

It was dark outside when he finished cleaning the cabin. He didn't have the time to clean as thoroughly in the bathroom. It and the outside would have to wait until she visited next time. Tonight was special. He must look his best. Standing in the shower cabin, feeling the ice cold water on his naked body, he felt even more excited than after he'd killed her mother and those men. Tonight was the start of his new life. He hoped that bitch Bodil was dead. That way, she'd never pester him again. Because of her poisonous mind he'd believed Astrid didn't care about him. He'd kill her if she meddled in his life again.

Exiting the shower cabin, he dried himself with the only towel, attempting to clean his hands and nails with a toothbrush. He brushed his thin gray hair, wishing it was shorter, but he told himself his daughter wouldn't care about such petty things. All she wanted was to meet and spend time with him. Laughing out loud, he looked around him, at the dirty room and window.

The snow was still falling, making the outdoors resemble a picture postcard. Humming an old nursery rhyme his mother had sung when he and Joel went to bed, preparing them for what their father was about to inflict on them, he thought *I'll kill her after Daniel and Joel. She doesn't deserve to live after turning a blind eye to what he did to us. We need a clean slate, no more pain and bad memories. No one will come between me and my daughter!*

Putting on the same dirty, smelly blue jeans, t-shirt, and clogs, he sat down at the table in the room and waited for her arrival.

When they arrived on the scene, Knudsen informed Arvid, "We've got everything under control, and we have no reason to suspect he's got someone in there with him. His old truck's parked in a side street off the main road. We managed to unlock it and found old blood stains which we will send to forensics to see if they match the Oslo victims' DNA."

"You and your men make me proud to be a policeman. Thank you so much for letting me be a part of this operation," Arvid responded.

Knudsen nodded and called Daniel on his mobile, inquiring where exactly he and Joel were hiding.

"We're behind the big black dustbins at the back of the cabin."

"Good. Whatever score you want to settle with him is out of question while she's inside with him; is that understood?"

"Don't worry, we wouldn't contemplate something so ludicrous. Joel wants to talk to you."

Arvid heard him say, "You'd better not risk her life! My brother's a psychopath, with nothing to lose if he suspects you've put her up to meeting him. If something bad happens to her, I'll never forgive you."

"That makes two of us. I and my officers are positioned outside. Just make sure the two of you don't reveal where you're hiding. If Aksel gets a hint you're out there, he'll put two and two together and kill you and her!"

"Sure. But if something bad happens to her before we can get to her, I'll hold you responsible, officer!" Joel's voice broke. "Let me talk to Arvid."

Knudsen handed the phone to Arvid, and Joel said, "Just promise me one thing: It's too late for regrets where my brother's concerned. If your only option is to shoot him, please get it over and done with as fast as you can, the same way as you'd kill an injured animal. He's too ill to understand what he's done and is about to do. As far as he's concerned he's done nothing wrong."

"I promise, unless we've no option but to shoot him in the legs or another part of his body first."

Knudsen took the phone back from Arvid and said to Joel, "Now, listen very carefully to what I'm about to tell you: Astrid's on her way to the cabin. She'll arrive in exactly five minutes. Don't do anything that might risk her life!"

Arvid's hands were shaking while he watched the girl get out of the car and slowly walk the short distance in the thick snow. He prayed nothing bad would happen to her inside the cabin. The last thing he'd asked her was if she was prepared to meet her father. She was shaking from the cold outside and eager to get it over and done with, but she assured him she'd be fine.

"Soon the man who killed my mother will be arrested and I'll be able to get on with my life."

Much too excited to sit at the table, Aksel paced the room and looked outside the window to see if she'd arrived. Everything was so quiet outside, almost as if he was the only person in the cabin in the entire forest. He was on the verge of calling her mobile when he heard a knock on the front door. Preparing to see and greet her, he looked outside to see if she was alone, then cautiously opened the door. "You came… Please come inside. I've waited so long to see you."

Feeling his ice cold hand on her face, she trembled. Forcing herself to say something, anything, she replied in a shaky voice, "I'm so pleased we finally get to meet, Far." Following him inside, eyes taking in the dirty room, she sat down opposite him at the chipped wooden table by the window.

"Let me take a closer look at you! You're prettier than your mother; she forbade me to see you. Ingrid was a bitch!"

"That's not true. She told me she wished the two of you could have stayed together, and I know how much she regretted keeping us apart from each other. I've reconciled myself with what happened and hope you will too. Can you do it, Far, for my sake?" She smiled reassuringly.

Watching his pale, drawn, unshaven face, the old scar she recalled when he visited her and her mother all those years ago on the left cheek, puffy eyes lighting up when staring at her, she thought he looked awful, the thin hair glued to his scalp and dirty clothes highlighting the scruffy man and sick mind.

"Of course I can! I'll do anything you want. Ingrid's dead; she can't come between us anymore." He touched her hand across the table. She cringed and withdrew from his touch before she could stop herself. She could see the agitation and suspicion rise in him immediately.

"Are you alright?" he asked, but his voice was cold and hostile. "I thought you wanted to spend time with me and be close. Are you hiding something from me?"

"Of course not! I'm so happy to be here with you, please don't stare at me like that." She felt the most fearful she'd ever been since finding out her mother died, but she reached out to touch his hand.

But it was too late. She could tell Aksel sensed she was lying to him. Pushing aside her hand, he got up from his chair, shouting "You're lying! Did the police put you up to this? Where are they? Don't pretend you don't know they're outside, preparing to arrest me!"

Before she could respond, Aksel grabbed her arm, holding it in a firm grip, then twisted it so hard she cried out in pain.

"Why are you hurting me? Please don't kill me!" She was too scared to stick with the psychiatrist's advice that she try to stay calm no matter how difficult.

"What makes you think I'll kill you? Who put such a crazy idea inside your head? Oh, I understand, someone's told you what to say! You've been coached to act and talk to make me think you care about me! Your appearance on TV, everything's a trap to trick me into coming forward! You little bitch! I wish I'd killed you with your mother!" Twisting her arm even harder, he watched her cry, begging him to let her go.

"I've got enough bullets in my gun to shoot you and Dan and my brother! My own brother left me just like everyone else."

Terrified he'd kill her there and then, Astrid sobbed hysterically, "I've not lied about wanting you to be part of my life. You've got to believe me!"

But no matter how hard she tried to convince him she cared, he just seemed to get angrier and angrier. Spitting in her face, he dragged her towards the window, opening it with one hand, shouting, "I know you're out there hiding from me! Unless you leave now, I'll shoot her in the head, and you'll have another body in the morgue!"

He tightened his grip on her arm, and she cried, "Please just leave, or he'll kill me!" Her grandfather was wrong, imagining he wouldn't see through her. Preparing herself for the inevitable, she cried so loudly she didn't hear footsteps behind them.

Grabbing Aksel's neck, Daniel placed a knife against his throat. "Let her go or I'll cut your throat!"

Stunned, Aksel froze, his grip loosening on her arm. He hissed at her, "You lied to me. All of you tricked me!" Screaming obscenities at them and the officers entering the cabin, followed by Joel, Knudsen and Arvid, he let go of her arm.

Making sure she was safe, Arvid watched two officers holding her on either side, taking her out of there. Following her outside, he held her close, crying, "I thought I would lose you, I'm so sorry for everything you've had to endure. You're safe now; no one will ever hurt you again."

Sobbing in his arms, Astrid said, "I thought he was going to kill me just like my mother! Please get me away from here now." Feeling an officer's hand on her shoulder, she heard Joel say, "You must let him escort you to Arvid's car and wait for us." Nodding, she felt his hand on hers and started to relax, walking the short distance. Shivering inside the car, she prayed her grandfather and friends would soon join her, thinking, *My father died a long time ago. The only thing that's left is a shell and sick mind.*

Inside the cabin, Arvid asked the other officers to leave. "I've got everything under control. Daniel and Joel will stay while I arrest him."

The officer in charge of security shook his head. "Are you sure that's wise? You're too close to the cases to think straight."

Arvid looked at Knudsen. "Please," he said, "I need to do this."

Knudsen looked at him long and hard, then nodded to the other officers to leave. "We'll return to the station. I'll expect you there soon." He turned and followed his colleagues out.

Arvid approached the killer, whom Daniel and Joel held on either side, and spat in his face. "You pathetic piece of shit! I couldn't care less about what happens to you. You've had a miserable life, but enduring your father's abuse doesn't excuse what you've done! You killed my daughter! Ingrid was my little girl and you shot her! You'll never get the chance to see my granddaughter again for as long as you live! Take him away from me and out of my sight!"

Watching the two men take him with them to the police car parked behind the back entrance, he took great pleasure in watching the pathetic excuse of a man attempting to break free from their strong grip on his neck and arms. But just as they were about to bundle him inside the car, Daniel slipped on the snow, losing his grip on the killer's arm.

Cutting loose from him, Aksel punched Joel hard in the face and tried to run away from them. He stumbled on a branch and fell to the ground. Twisting his right leg he cried out in pain. Daniel leaped on him and pushed his face deep down in the cold snow, screaming, "I ought to shoot you in the back just like you did to those people!"

159

He pulled out a gun from his inside jacket pocket. It was the same gun Aksel had threatened to use on Astrid. He was about to pull the trigger when someone else beat him to it, firing the fatal shot. Aksel's head was blown to pieces and his blood soaked the snow.

Half an hour later, the forensic team arrived to examine the body and scene, informing Arvid it would take some time before they'd bring the body to the morgue. It was over. Aksel was dead and Bodil would spend the rest of her life in prison.

Walking towards his car and seeing his granddaughter sitting inside, alive and well, he thanked his lucky stars she hadn't been killed. Turning to look at the two men behind him, he said, "I guess you need time on your own. I'll drive Astrid home. The station can wait until the morning."

Joel asked, "Will you report me for shooting him?"

Shaking his head, Arvid replied kindly, "Never. Aksel had it coming. You did the right thing, acting in self-defense. At least now, he won't be locked up in a psychiatric clinic in a straitjacket. You wanted him to die quickly and now you've got your wish. I'll make sure you won't pay for what you did. Relax, you've nothing to worry about."

Watching them drive away, Daniel put a hand on Joel's shoulder. "I know you feel bad right now and will for some time but you did the right thing."

"If what you say is true how come I feel so upset?" His eyes were brimming with tears. "Our so-called parents destroyed him, Daniel. I'll always regret leaving him behind. He never stood a chance."

"I feel the same way about Ingrid. We must try to live with our mistakes and put the past behind us."

* * * *

Two months later, three people visited Ingrid's grave in a small chapel in Sandviken. Placing a single red rose on her coffin, Daniel held Astrid close to him, whispering in her ear, "I've fallen in love with you, honey. Your mother meant a lot to me and now we've got the opportunity to rebuild our lives properly. Will you accompany me on the journey?"

Touching his face, Astrid bowed her head. "I've fallen in love with you too. Let's make a pact to not revisit the past except the good times."

Happy the people he cared about most had found happiness with each other, Joel said, "I've had closure with my past. Will you sell Holst Enterprises? I can't imagine you continuing working like you did."

Daniel shrugged. "I've given away a big part of the profits to two charities. Both are close to my heart: preventing domestic abuse and helping to prevent other kids from enduring what we did. Aksel's life could have turned out differently if someone gave a damn about what happened to him and us. From now on, I'll devote time to being with the woman I love. I've set you up for life; it's the least I can do for my best and most loyal friend."

Leaving the chapel, Astrid knew she'd at long last found the inner peace she needed to be happy and fulfilled. Daniel was the last man she'd imagined falling in love with, but it had happened and Joel had turned out to be the best uncle she could ever have wished for. She and Arvid were getting closer and as she turned to look at her mother's grave, she whispered, "Rest in peace, Mor. Your little girl's safe."

Thank you for reading *One Fatal Night*. I hope you enjoyed it. If so, please do go to Amazon and/or Goodreads and leave a rating and review to let others know that you would recommend it.

Join my mailing list.
If you want to know more about me and my writing and be kept up to date about future books coming soon, you can sign up to the newsletter on my website at:

www.helenefermont.com

Or follow me on one or more of the following social media platforms:

http://www.twitter.com/helenefermont
http://www.facebook.com/helenefermontauthor
http://www.instagram.com/helenefermont

With best wishes always, Hélene x

Because of You

by Hélene Fermont

How desperate are you to get the love of your life?

The moment Ben Isaacs lays eyes on nineteen-year-old Hannah Stein, he knows their connection will last forever. Yet the impressionable Swedish beauty is entangled with immoral womaniser, Mark Copeck, and due to return home to her native Malmö.

Meanwhile, wealthy Vanessa Westbrook will stop at nothing to claim Isaacs as her own, and sets in motion a series of events that will change the course of all four lives irrevocably.

Spanning three turbulent decades from the heady era of the 1970s London club scene to the striking backdrop of modern-day Limhamn, *Because of You* explores the true meaning of enduring love, fidelity and fate, as two polar opposite women shape the destinies of all those they hold dear.

We Never Said Goodbye

by Hélene Fermont

Is it ever too late to start again?

When Louise is dumped by Mike on their twentieth wedding anniversary, she faces the daunting task of picking up the pieces of her life. She can either choose to persevere in her adopted hometown of London, bolstered by dear friends and the fashion business she loves, or return to her native Sweden alone. Can she find happiness with an old flame in a city she avoided for two decades? Or will her ex's violent, criminal past haunt her forever?

As Mike becomes increasingly unhinged, the choices Louise makes could prove fatal. Will she ever be able to say goodbye to the past and start afresh?

His Guilty Secret

by Hélène Fermont

When Jacques's body is discovered in a hotel room his wife, Patricia, suspects he has been hiding something from her.

Why was he found naked and who is the woman that visited his grave on the day of the funeral? Significantly, who is the unnamed beneficiary Jacques has left a large sum of money to in his will, and what is the reason her best friend, and Jacques's sister, Coco, refused to tell her what he confided in her?

As one revelation after another is revealed, Patricia is yet to discover her husband's biggest secret, and, what ultimately killed him.

His Guilty Secret is an examination of the tangled bonds between siblings, the lengths we go to in protecting our wrongdoings, and the enduring psychological effect this has on the innocent…and the not so innocent.

Who's Sorry Now?

By Hélene Fermont

Who's Sorry Now? is about love, betrayal and dreams.

Do we really know the people we love?

Can love be rekindled?

Do dreams come true?

The truth always comes out in the end.

A collection of four crime and romance stories.

ABOUT THE AUTHOR

Born into a bilingual family (Swedish/English), Hélene Fermont enjoyed an idyllic childhood on the outskirts of Malmö, Sweden's third largest city and major cultural hub. Growing up in the 1970s, she had a brief musical career on Swedish TV and radio prior to pursuing a career in teaching and a practising psychologist. Hélene lived in London for over 20 years but has recently returned to Sweden. She is currently working on her fifth novel, *The Matchmaker*.

Printed in Poland
by Amazon Fulfillment
Poland Sp. z o.o., Wrocław

62075316R00101